THE Boyfriend CLUB

WHERE **SCENES** DO COME TRUE...

by

Angie Lee

Also by Angie Lee

The Window
One Last Lie
The Window Duet Special Edition

Something Borrowed: a Haunted Novella

This book is dedicated to all the
"Book Boyfriend" addicts.
If your heart has ever been stolen by a character
and you desperately wished they were real…

This one's for you.

Acknowledgements

I started writing in 2022, and in the few short years since then, I've met so many wonderful people, other authors, and readers. I owe them endless thanks.

First to my daughter-in-law, whose love of book boyfriends inspired The Boyfriend Club.

To the members of The Bookish Retreat, Mary, Ellie, Aimee, Jordan, Sharecia, and Erin, to name just a few, and especially Lindsey Nicole. All of you have supported and cheered me on every step of the way, and I appreciate it from the bottom of my heart. Even though I haven't met any of you in real life, I consider you all friends.

To two of my favorite readers, Megan Morales, and Kristy Jonkers. You two have made me feel like what I write is worth reading.

To Wanda Jean, for your priceless insight on dating apps.

I'd like to send a special thank you to Margaux Hamilton, whose beautiful name I've fallen in love with. Luckily, Margaux has graciously given me permission to use it in my next book.

About the Author

Angie Lee is the first-place winner of Miss Stacey's second-grade poetry contest. She beat out the competition with a poem about kites, taking the grand prize of one large gold star sticker.

She lives in a tiny Louisiana town with her husband and their dog.

Angie loves writing but has found that her real talent lies in procrastinating. In her free time, Angie enjoys using a Magic 8 Ball to make tough life decisions.

Chapter 1

Up In Flames

I think I'm drunk.

"I think you're drunk!" My sister's shout comes through the open patio door leading to the living room, where she's made herself home on my sofa. She probably has her shoes up on the cream-colored cushions, too, but I can't bring myself to care right now.

Being drunk feels… good. I should do this again. Soon.

"It feels good, doesn't it?" Lindsey's words are a bit more slurred with each passing minute.

Am I speaking out loud? I could have sworn I was just thinking those things. I reach up to make sure my lips aren't moving, and nope, they're not. She must be reading my mind.

Anyway, I never thought I'd be standing barefoot in my backyard wearing my wedding veil, a decades-old pair of Halloween pajamas, and a wine bottle in hand, but here we are. The tiny ghosts floating across my flannel pants seem to dance in the light of the flames. Or maybe I've progressed to hallucinations.

I take another healthy swig straight from the bottle as I watch my custom wedding dress cook to an excellent medium-well on the barbeque smoking in the corner of the yard. Through the fog, I vaguely wonder if toxic chemicals are being released into the air, but then I realize I don't care about that either, or much of anything at this moment.

I feel a particularly perverse pleasure as I watch the glittering hand-sewn beads scattered across the bodice melt in the flames. I push the antique veil from my face and behind my shoulders, out of the way to not impede my front-row view of the sixteen-thousand-dollar couture dress burning.

It's such a pity I never got to wear it, as it was quite literally made for me and fit like a ridiculously expensive, handmade glove.

Once the dress is all but ashes, I remove the veil from my head and add it to the smoldering pile of remaining fabric. Another overly generous squirt of lighter fluid and it's reduced to smoking lace and tulle.

Belatedly, I wonder if I should have sent the dress to a consignment store or even a pawn shop. I didn't pay for it, but I could have gotten a little compensation for my pain and suffering.

Oh, well. Too late now.

Another long gulp from the wine bottle, and I realize, with no small measure of sadness, the damn thing is nearly empty. Dropping the bottle on the grass, I strip off my smoke-soaked pants and tank and strut back into the house, naked as the day I came into this world.

My little sister, Lindsey, is splayed out on the sofa, *her shoes on*, and her half-empty bottle clutched loosely in her fist. With a struggle, she opens one eye when she hears me come in.

"Ish it done?' she slurs, struggling to sit up. "Ish Been-a-dick dead and buried?" Despite the gravity of my current situation, I laugh at her nickname for my fiancé… I mean, EX-fiancé, as of a handful of hours ago.

She opens the other eye, looks me over, and grimaces. "Why are you naked?"

Unconcerned, I wander over to the other end of the sofa and shove Lindsey's legs to the side, making room for myself. Grabbing a blanket to cover up my most significant bits, I nod.

"Yep. Ashes to ashes and all that. Also, mind your own business. By the way, do you know about forty-two percent of marriages end in divorce?"

Here's a thing to know about me: When I'm sad, on edge, or angry, I spout useless facts. Mostly, the kind of things no one really needs to know but that live rent-free in my head. It's a nervous tick of sorts.

"Stop that." A bit more sober now, my sister leans over and puts her head on my shoulder, giving me an affectionate nudge. "You know he was never good enough for you, right?"

I know. I do know, but that doesn't make it hurt less.

As though reading my mind again, she goes on, sitting up and tucking her legs beneath herself.

"Now that you're done sacrificing your dress to the gods, we've got to decide on some epic revenge plan. There's no way Dick is going to get away with this. If he thinks he's going to ride off into the sunset with the whore formerly known as your wedding planner, he's got another thing coming."

Her words make me wince, but they're nothing less than the truth. Ben did abandon me hours before we were due to say our vows—and yes, for our wedding planner, no less. A useless fact pops into my mind with perfect timing.

"It's think, not thing," I correct.

"What?"

"Another *think* coming. It's a common misconception that it's *thing*. So common, in fact, it's been widely accepted as correct."

Lindsey rolls her eyes and chooses not to respond.

"Anyway, I just thought of something we could do to get him back," she says, her face flushed with excitement and too much alcohol.

"I read this story once about a woman whose husband put her out of the house and moved his girlfriend in, so she snuck in while they were sleeping and stuffed raw shrimp in all his curtain rods and after days of not being able to find the source of the smell, he sold the house back to the wife for pennies on the dollar."

"Come on, Lin. That did not happen." Despite myself, I giggle at the image of a man wandering his house, sniffing the air in confusion.

"Yes, it did! I saw it online. Or on the news. Or maybe somebody told me the story. I don't remember; that's not the point! The point is, the scorned woman moved back in, threw out the stinking curtain rods, and lived happily ever after."

Inspired, my red wine-soaked brain tries to imagine other fun revenge ideas.

"Ooh, I know! Nair in his shampoo bottle! You know how much Ben loves his hair!" We both double over with laughter. "Can you imagine the look on his face when he has his hands full of those luscious locks?"

I have to admit, that is rather genius. Ben is obsessive about how his hair looks. He cannot pass a mirror without checking to make sure every strand is in place and behaving.

Lindsey tries to catch her breath before offering the next idea. "Magazines. That is the answer."

I'm confused. "Magazines? How do you use those for revenge?" I ask.

"Oh, my sweet sister. Take my hand, and let me lead you into the darkness. You subscribe to questionable magazines in his name, but… wait for it…. have them sent to his office *and* his mother's house!"

We both squeal like a couple of teenagers. I like this even more than the Nair idea.

"Hell has no fury…" Lindsey starts.

"Hath." I correct without meaning to. Schoolteacher habits die hard.

"What?"

"It's *hath*, not *has*."

My poor sister is confused. "What the hell is a *hath*?"

I'm stumped and say so. "I actually… don't have a clue."

And we break into giggles again. I make a mental note to look into the word 'hath' when I'm sober again.

We stay up for hours, each revenge plot becoming increasingly outrageous and unlikely. At one point, we find a notebook and pen and fill the pages with ideas, everything from sending penis-shaped glitter bombs to Ben's office to covering his car with Post-It notes to sending ED literature and meds to his house and office. My favorite part of the night is the plot which involves pouring tons of instant mashed potatoes all over his car and lawn right before it rains.

My sister falls asleep before I do, and hours later, I'm still awake and regrettably sober. Watching the sunrise through the gap in the living room curtains, I feel peace covering me like a warm blanket. The next phase of my life is about to begin, and I can't wait to see what it brings.

Chapter 2

A Perfect Match?

I imagine you're curious to know what led up to me burning my wedding dress in the backyard so I won't keep you in suspense.

As I mentioned, the short version is that my fiance left me for the wedding planner—after I caught them together.

More details, you say? Okay. If you're sure you want the whole sordid story…

It went something like this:

His name is Benedict Thompson, but he likes to be called Ben. We'll stick with Ben, or maybe Dick, for the sake of this story, but thanks to Lindsey, he'll forever be known to the two of us as Been-a-Dick.

Dick…*BEN* is one of *the* Thompsons, if you know what I mean. If you don't, it means that his family owns most of the more upscale hotels in the New Orleans area. His mother is also from a long line of restaurateurs, so I guess you could say his parents were a match made in service industry heaven.

Not so much Ben and me.

At first, the relationship seemed perfect. Ben, the heir to the hotel chain throne, swooped in and swept me, a small-town girl and school-teacher, off my feet and into a whirlwind romance. We met at the library, which made my book-loving heart melt. Later, I'd find out that his parents had given him an ultimatum, half of which was to "find a nice girl and settle down or else..." and I fit the bill.

I was wined and dined, and a mere three months after we met, I was de-flowered.

I'd later come to realize that it was a disappointing experience. To put it nicely, if I had to write a book about it, it'd be a real short story.

The next thing I know, I'm engaged and dropped in the middle of the wedding plans Ben's mother, Rebecca, was making for me.

That's right. Rebecca was in charge of everything, from the style and designer of my dress to the venue and color of my attendants' dresses.

She and the aforementioned whore-of-a-wedding-planner, Sasha (who was also chosen by Rebecca), just told me where to go and when to be there, and I complied. I put my foot down when they tried to choose my bridesmaids, only wanting Lindsey and Ellie, my best friend from college, at my side.

To keep the peace, I let Rebecca do whatever else she wanted with the plans. None of it mattered; I thought I was in love with Ben and was looking forward to getting to the other side of the wedding day.

Fast forward to the night of our rehearsal dinner.

It was a dark and rainy night…

I'm just kidding.

It was a gorgeous, perfect spring evening, with low humidity and clear skies, as though Ben's mother had ordered it according to her exact specifications.

Just like the engagement party a month before, the rehearsal dinner was lavish. At one of Ben's family hotels, obviously.

Only the best of everything would do for Ben and his parents. After we'd pretended to walk down the aisle and said our practice vows, the wedding party and a dozen others that had been invited moved to the adjoining overdecorated banquet room for a light dinner and cocktails. Nothing on the menu was my choice.

It was all picture-perfect. The imported French vanilla & lavender candles flickered softly, expensive French champagne flowed, and the guests seemed to be having a wonderful time.

I'd never felt so out of place and awkward in my life. It may as well have been someone else's party. In fact, a few guests seemed not to realize I was the bride; one older lady asked me to refill her glass.

As though she heard me thinking these negative thoughts, Ben's mother looked over and caught my eye. She cast a critical glance over my dress. I think she was making sure none of my undergarments were showing or that I'd otherwise done something to embarrass her.

I wondered how she'd feel if I'd reached up my butt and pulled out the torture device, also known as shapewear.

After she nodded her approval and moved on to her next group of guests, I made a few slow loops around the room, smiling at a few of them I'd met before, but was mostly ignored. That was fine by me; I figured I'd never see most of these people again after the wedding tomorrow.

Uniform-clad waiters floated by but I had no appetite. There were at least a dozen fancy finger foods I could hardly pronounce the name of being passed around on silver trays and a golden, sparkling champagne tower in the middle of the room.

So much waste. The excess made me cringe, as I tend to like things on the simpler side, but I tried to keep smiling as I accepted congratulations from people I'd never met and honestly hoped to never have to speak to again.

Ellie had been unable to make it, as her little girl had the stomach flu, so it was just me and Lindsey from our side. Our parents had both passed away years before, Dad first (heart attack) and Mom not long after (cancer). I had a few cousins scattered around in different states, but no one nearby.

As I sweated in my itchy, too-tight lace dress, clutching my almost full champagne flute, I wondered what my solid, middle-class, down-to-earth parents would have thought about this overdone affair.

Feeling a little lonely on my own and unsure where Ben had gone, I searched the room for Lindsey to ask her opinion and found her flirting with the bartender in the back corner.

Smiling to myself, I decided not to interrupt her fun and headed for the ladies' room to check for sweat stains on my ridiculous dress.

Which is just about when it all went to hell.

Chapter 3

Bathroom Break(up)

It should have been as simple as a quick trip to the restroom, a cursory hair and makeup check, and ensuring my dress was in place. I'd gone to one on the far side of the building to get away from everyone for a minute.

It's no big deal. People do it every day—in and out of the restroom without incident, right?

Nope… that's not what happened this time.

Alone in the deserted hallway, I pushed open the restroom door and stepped inside, pausing as I heard what I thought was a man's chuckle. Leaning back, I checked the gender sign on the front side of the door to make sure I hadn't gone into the wrong one, then clearly heard a woman's giggle.

Intrigued, I shut the door softly behind me and tiptoed towards the mirrors. In the last stall at the end of the row, I could see two sets of shoes peeking underneath the half walls, a man's and a woman's.

Well, wasn't that something? Those were undoubtedly my wedding planner's shoes. I'd recognize them anywhere.

During our wedding planning meetings, Sasha always wore little black dresses, each cut differently, but her choice of shoes was always interesting. She favored bold styles in outrageous colors. When we'd arrived tonight, I noticed she had chosen a pair of purple suede spike heels with gladiator straps wrapping up her calves.

Did you know that wearing high heels for long periods of time can shorten your calves?

I glanced down at my sensible kitten heels, then turned to make a quiet exit, making as little noise as possible. There was no need to disturb Sasha and whoever she was with. She'd made it clear more than once that she was single and looking, and I had no desire to spoil her fun either. I figured one of us should enjoy the party, and I sure wasn't.

Two paces from the door, I heard *my fiance* say, "You're going to have to stop moving around if you expect me to undo these tiny buttons." Another giggle from the homewrecker.

I must have gasped more loudly than I realized because the cheater and the slut both went quiet, no doubt at a loss about what to do now that they'd been busted doing *whatever* in a dirty bathroom stall at a wedding rehearsal where he was the groom and she the wedding planner.

The silence drug on for what felt like an hour, but was probably only a few seconds, until the hussy dared speak. "Is someone out there?" Her voice had changed from its usual loud assertiveness to that of a kid caught with her hand in the cookie jar.

I stayed silent, my mind reeling. My husband-to-be was… I wasn't sure what exactly was going on with the wedding planner. Whatever it was, it wasn't good. I mean, what happened to the girl code?

I glanced down at my watch to note the time as I waited to see what would happen next—relationship time of death: 6:47 p.m.

Surprisingly, I decided I was content to wait them out. I had nothing but time, and it would be impossible for them to leave the restroom without being exposed.

They were the first to break.

"Do you think they're still out there?" The ho asked this in a stage whisper.

"Did you hear the door open?" replied the pretender.

"Well, we can't just stay in here." Again from the slut.

"Okay, you go first and see if they're gone," suggested the liar, showing how much of a coward he was, totally willing to throw his sidepiece to the wolves… or me.

Still, I waited.

A whole minute passed before something finally happened.

The lock sliding from its home sounded like a gunshot in the otherwise silent room, and the door to the stall creaked open slowly.

The tramp stuck her head out, and I waited until her eyes met mine to speak.

"Hey, Sasha, who you got in there?'

Things happened quickly after that.

Before the tart could answer me, a masculine hand reached out of the stall and gave Sasha a shove as though he was trying to put distance between them just in case I hadn't noticed they were together.

Hey, I said he was rich, not bright.

She took a step to steady herself and slipped in a little puddle of water on the ceramic floor. Her legs shot out from under her, and down she went, arms flailing, hands grasping for something on which to catch herself.

But it didn't end with her just falling to the floor. Not even close.

The karma gods were either smiling at me or frowning at her; who knows?

With a sickening crack, her chin hit the porcelain rim of the nearest sink. With a yelp, she slid to the floor, landing face-first on the tile, and only then did she stop moving.

Ouch. And also, gross.

In addition to the blood and bruises, when she woke up, she'd be regretting her decision to go commando tonight.

Dick was frozen half in and half out of the stall, watching in horror as Sasha performed her macabre dance routine.

Only when she failed to get up did he finally look at me, his ordinarily tan complexion turning a strange grayish color.

"Is she… dead?" His voice held a strange mix of hope and dread, with a bit of emphasis on the hope.

Incredulous, I gaped at the philanderer. "That's your main concern right now? What about the fact that I just caught you with our wedding planner?"

Exasperated, I stepped over to the pile of limbs on the floor, leaned down, and pressed two fingers to her carotid artery.

Still beating, strong and steady. Unfortunately, despite the trickles of blood running from her nose and mouth, she was alive, just knocked out. From what I could see, her front teeth were chipped, and I wasn't even a little mad about it.

Dick reached out for me, his filthy, cheating hands raised in supplication. "Haley… it's not what you think."

I stepped away from both of them and out of his reach. "It's *exactly* what I think, and we're over."

Pulling my phone from my clutch, I snapped a quick picture of the harlot lying on the floor and left without another word, leaving Dick flustered and stuttering behind me.

Chapter 4

Mother Does Not Know Best

There was no spectacular exit, no tears or shouting.

After leaving the restroom, I found Lindsey where I'd last seen her, chatting up the cutie behind the bar. I whispered in her ear that I needed to leave immediately and bless her heart, she asked no questions. We were out the door and speeding away from the reception hall in less than two minutes.

We stayed quiet on the way home, her knowing instinctually that I wasn't ready to talk. When we arrived at my house, my sweet sister tucked me into bed with the promise we'd talk the next day and made herself a bed on the sofa for the night.

I want to say I was heartbroken, but if I'm completely honest with you and myself, Been-a-Dick was a bundle of walking red flags that I chose to ignore, the least of which was his relationship with his mother.

In truth, it all happened so quickly that I didn't give myself much time to second-guess my romance and quick engagement. I think deep down, I felt that at my age, I should have already been married with children, and Dick was the key to those things. He had a need that I fit, and he fit a need for me.

Should haves would do me no good, I thought as I finally fell asleep that night.

On the morning of what would have been my wedding day, I woke up to a half dozen messages, mainly from the lying dirtbag.

Please pick up the phone. We have to talk. Mother is upset and wants to sit down with both of us this morning so we can figure out where to go from here.

I chuckled. Not a chance in hell.

He and his mother could go heck themselves.

> *Haley, you're overreacting. Sasha meant nothing to me. She just had this way about her, you know? I couldn't help myself.*

He couldn't *help* himself? Was that supposed to make me feel better?

> *I know you're getting my messages, Haley. You never turn your phone off. Don't you think you're overreacting just a bit? She and I were only together three times. Well, maybe five. And technically, it's not cheating because we aren't married yet. You know I would never have done this after the wedding! Please call me back. This is ridiculous. Your behavior is extremely unbecoming.*

No, clearly *that* was the one that was supposed to make everything okay.

I decided not to answer and deleted all his messages. That felt damn good, so I removed all his photos and pictures of the two of us from my social media and changed my Relationship Status to *Single*. As to his texts, I wouldn't be sitting down with either of them. Dick and his mother could explain to everyone why there'd be no wedding.

A few minutes later, inspiration struck. I changed my mind and decided to send one text—but not to Ben.

To Ben's mother, I forwarded the photo of Sasha knocked out on the floor in the bathroom. In the picture, you could see Ben's mouth hanging open in shock as he stared, horrified, down at his unconscious, bloody paramour.

That should give the lying dirtbag and his mother something to talk about.

Lindsey and I spent the day with our phones off, watching chick flicks and only answering the door for the three food deliveries we ordered. A time like this called for Mexican, Chinese, *and* Italian. She'd also had a courier bring a deluxe-sized box of assorted chocolates and pastries for dessert.

Between courses, I again pulled out the photo I'd taken of Sasha for our viewing pleasure.

Later that night, she and I brought out the wine, and well, you know what happened then.

Chapter 5

A Little Self-Care

Ending an engagement should have been a bigger deal than it was. For me, at least.

I realized that I was not, in fact, sad about losing Ben. And I was definitely glad to be rid of his mother.

Sure, my pride was hurt to some degree, but it was more the idea of what we could have had that I grieved. I did want marriage, children, and the whole white picket fence package.

I just didn't want it with Ben. The thing was, having only been with him, I wasn't sure what I wanted in a man or a relationship.

I didn't realize that soon I'd be handed a golden opportunity to find out.

The day after the dress burning, Lindsey had to leave to return to work. I'd miss her, but she had her own life to get on with. Luckily, I was off since I was supposed to be on my honeymoon.

I took the whole day to pull myself together and handle whatever matters needed my attention.

First, I called my boss to let her know I wouldn't need that two weeks off for my honeymoon after all. After offering her condolences and asking some not-so-subtle questions, she told me to take three days off. Then we hung up, and I unpacked my suitcases and put my things away. Once my closet was back in order, I grabbed a notebook and made a list of gifts that needed to be returned and to whom.

That done, I dressed and drove downtown to the jeweler where I'd purchased Ben's wedding band a few weeks before.

The nice man at the counter refunded my money, no questions asked.

I guess they were used to broken engagements.

I decided to grab a super-fattening, cream-and-sugar-laden Frappuccino and then head to my favorite bookstore.

The quaint, downtown shop was my happy place. I'd found it by accident a few months back, and it had become one of my favorite places to spend my free time. The serenity, the quiet, and the smell of books surrounding me from every side were my go-to for relaxation.

Thanks to the ring refund, I had a handful of crisp bills burning a hole in my pocket.

I had been thinking all day that it might also be time for me to take a little trip to another kind of shop, the kind I'd never been brave enough to venture into, but I was single now and probably would be for a while. Reinforcements might be necessary.

As I slowly walked the pathway up to the shop, I admired the exterior.

It was a cottage-style building designed to make you feel like you were coming home, and it worked. It didn't hurt that there was always a tray of warm, fresh-baked cookies on the counter where you checked out your purchases. As a bonus, I had an online account with the store, where I could review books I'd read, send messages to authors, and keep a wish list of books I was interested in reading.

Inside, I smiled at the other best thing about this place.

Piper, the gorgeous raven-haired owner of the establishment, sat behind the counter, checking things off on a clipboard. Her long red nails caught my eye, and I made a mental note to treat myself to a manicure with whatever money was left over after this little shopping trip.

Piper and I had become friendly over the previous few months, and I'd told her all about Ben and the wedding plans.

"Hey, sweetie! How are ya?" She winked and motioned me over with one graceful wave of her hand.

Her smile warmed me as always, so I wandered over to the counter to chat. I had nothing but time to kill, and money to burn.

"I've been better, honestly," I replied, raising my left hand and wiggling my empty ring finger.

Piper's eyes grew wide, and she gasped, "Oh, no! What happened, honey?"

"The wedding planner," I said dryly, rolling my eyes.

"The wedding planner? You didn't like her? You couldn't just find another one?" Piper sounded as bewildered as I'd felt hearing Ben's voice coming from the bathroom stall.

"Well, it wasn't so much that I didn't like her. It's that Ben liked her *too* much."

Piper's eyes narrowed, and her hands curled into fists.

It struck me at that moment that I never wanted this woman mad at me.

"Tell me everything."

When I was done relaying the whole ugly story, to my surprise, Piper didn't blow up. She didn't call him names or threaten to hurt him like I'd thought she would. I was a little disappointed, honestly.

Instead, she gazed at me silently for a minute, one long red fingernail tapping against her perfectly painted lips.

Just as I was about to ask her what she was thinking, she reached out and put her hand on my wrist.

"Haley, do you believe in fate?"

Did I? I wasn't sure, and I said so.

"I don't know if I do or not… Why do you ask?"

"I want you to do something for me just because I'm asking you to. Okay?"

Expecting a pep talk about self-care and how I shouldn't blame myself, I suppressed an eye roll and agreed. "Okay. Sure."

"Listen carefully. There's something I want you to see, so come back tonight at eight, and promise me you'll keep an open mind?"

She phrased the last bit like a question, and I admit I was intrigued. "But you close at seven. Why would I come after closing?"

"Just trust me. The door will be unlocked." She smiled reassuringly. "We're having a sort of… club meeting, I guess you could call it."

Book club? I was in. I didn't understand the secrecy or the after-hours part, but whatever. It's not like I had anything else to do.

Chapter 6

What Happens After Dark

I was nervous while getting dressed. Trepida-tion had me second-guessing myself and my decision to go along with whatever Piper was being so cagey about.

I'd turned it around in my mind and couldn't figure out why Piper wouldn't just tell me what the club was about or why they met after closing time. Guess I'd find out soon enough.

I put on my favorite jeans, a white V-neck tee, and my old, battered leather jacket to boost my courage. A little lip gloss and a light swipe of mascara were all the makeup I wanted. A comfy pair of boots, and I was ready.

I thought about calling Lindsey to fill her in on what I was up to, but then I remembered how vague Piper was about the club meeting and decided to keep the night's events to my- self until I knew more. Maybe once I was "in" the club, I could invite her and Ellie, and we'd make a regular girls' night out of it, maybe with dinner and drinks afterwards.

After all, it was a book club, so how bad could it be?

The porch light over the bookshop's door was lit, but no other light came from the windows.

For the second time that day, I walked up to the door, but before I could turn the knob, the door swung inward, revealing Piper, grinning from ear to ear.

She'd changed into a red, flowy dress with silver dangling earrings, and she looked stun- ning. I wondered if I'd underdressed, but she hadn't said anything about a dress code.

"Haley, you came! I'm so glad!" She pulled me in for a quick, tight hug and then released me, keeping her grip on my hand as she led me past the counter, down a darkened aisle, and to a door that read "Employees Only Beyond This Point."

Piper tugged me through the door and into the room beyond. Expecting an office or employee break room, I was surprised to find myself in a nicely appointed waiting room. It reminded me a lot of a nicer doctor or dentist's office.

I wasn't alone. Four other women were sitting in comfortable-looking chairs set around the room in a circular pattern, with a coffee table in the middle. The room was softly lit by standing lamps in each corner, and across from the door we came through, there was a low wooden table serving as a bar with coffee, bottled water, tea, and a tray of what looked like Piper's homemade cookies.

Gesturing towards one of the only two empty chairs, Piper invited me to sit. "Make yourself at home; I'll be back to get you in a few. There's snacks and water on that table if you'd like. Help yourself."

Get me?

Before I could ask any questions, she disappeared through an unmarked door at the room's far end.

The Present

Chapter 7

Smut Club

I'm officially nervous now; my earlier tension has amplified. Have I marched myself into a sex trafficking scheme? Or maybe one of those hidden camera TV shows?

I force myself to stop looking for tiny camera lenses on the ceiling and glance around at the other people in the room.

Thankfully, none of them are looking back. The other women are engrossed in their separate activities: two are reading books and one is scrolling through her phone. The last, I notice, is biting her nails as she focuses on the door Piper disappeared through.

That doesn't help to calm the butterflies in my stomach at all. Trying to be rational, I decide she's probably new to the club, like me, and anxious about meeting new people.

The other women in the room all seem to be around my age—late twenties, maybe early thirties. I wish I were brave enough to ask one of them what's happening here, but I'm not.

Thankfully, I don't have to think about it long because the door opens again, and Piper sticks her head out, looking towards the anxious-seeming girl.

"Charlotte, are you ready, honey?" Piper speaks gently to the girl, her voice calm and soothing.

"Um… yes?" stutters Charlotte, her cheeks turning a near-neon shade of pink. Piper walks over, takes Charlotte by the hand, and leads her back to the door.

"Sweetheart, it's okay. We went over this yesterday, remember? You don't have to do anything you don't want to, okay? You're free to leave whenever you like, including right now, if you aren't ready."

Charlotte's indecision is obvious. She glances at the entry door and then at the one Piper just emerged from.

I'm captivated, dying to know what Charlotte is so worried about, needing to know what's behind that door.

Will she stay or go?

The other women don't even look up from their books and phones. It's becoming clear that whatever happens to the members of this "club" isn't scary.

And Charlotte doesn't look frightened; she seems shy. I watch as she makes up her mind and nods, indicating to Piper that she's ready for whatever it is, and they disappear back through the same door.

My imagination runs wild. Is this a club for a particular type of book?

I guess here's where I admit that I love romance books, and if they're spicy, that's even better.

Don't get me wrong, I'm fully aware that most real-life men aren't like the ones in books, but a girl can dream, right?

I bet that's what this is—just a group of women who read spicy books and then get together to talk about them.

It's a smut club.

Yep. I'm absolutely going to invite Lindsey and Ellie.

Without meaning to, I let out a little giggle, and the blonde girl reading across from me looks up at the sound. She catches my eye and smiles before looking back down at her page.

My curiosity grows, along with a burgeoning feeling of excitement. I'm ready to go through the door, regardless of what's on the other side.

There's no chance of me changing my mind and leaving.

Thirty minutes, which feel more like ninety, pass before any more doors open.

When Piper finally comes out, looking down at her phone, I let out a breath and send up a little prayer to whoever might be listening.

Please pick me, please pick me.

She doesn't.

"Erin? Come on through, darling."

Dammit.

The blonde girl who smiled at me earlier closes her book, slides it into her purse, and stands. After smoothing her already perfect hair with her hands, she confidently follows Piper back through the door. But before it closes, Piper sticks her head out and looks directly at me.

"Get ready, Haley, you're next." A saucy wink and she's gone.

Chapter 8

By Invitation Only

I've been sitting on the edge of my seat for the last ten minutes. I've checked my phone a dozen times, filed off a hangnail, counted the tiles in the ceiling, and am about to start pacing a hole in the floor when finally, that damn door opens, and Piper calls my name.

"Okay, Haley, you ready?"

Am I? I don't know.

"Yep!" I aim for light and breezy, but it morphs into an unladylike squeak.

No matter. I'm nervous, excited, intrigued, and a bunch of other adjectives.

I get up and gather my things, moving toward where Piper waits, a slight smile on her pretty face. Like the blonde before me, I attempt a confident stride but only manage a medium grimace and clumsy stumble.

Piper gives me a knowing grin and reaches for my elbow, gently ushering me through the door and into the next room.

We step inside, and she closes the door softly behind us. I glance around, trying to take in as much as I can.

It's another average-sized room. Two comfortable-looking chairs surround a small bistro-style table, which sits upon a large oval rug in muted colors. A tall wooden filing cabinet is tucked in a corner, and other than a laptop closed on the table, the room has only one other noticeable feature.

The walls hold a gallery of book covers—small, large, black-and-white, and full-color. There must be a hundred or more, beautifully framed in groupings on all four walls. Piper gestures to one chair and arranges herself in another, and I scan as many as I can while settling into my own.

Some of the covers are photographs, others digital art or hand-drawn, some with authors I recognize, and the rest I've never heard of. But all the book covers have one thing in common.

They're all romance reads, some light spice, some darker. My gaze catches on the dark and dramatic covers of a series of three books I finished just a few weeks ago, and I feel the heat rush to my cheeks as I remember a few specific scenes that are still living rent-free in my head.

A tiny spark of triumph makes me grin because now I'm positive I've figured it out. This is almost certainly a smut club, and I want in. Boy, do I have a lot to say about *that* particular trilogy.

Finally, I manage to tear my eyes away from the walls and focus on Piper who is patiently waiting for my attention. She's reclined in her seat, looking like she has all the time in the world.

I set my bag on the floor beside my chair and get comfortable, completely at ease now that the mystery has been solved.

"I know what this is, and I'm in."

Piper smirks. "You think so?"

"Yep. It's a spicy book club." I don't want to say smut club for some reason. "Why all the secrecy, though?"

Piper considers before answering. "You're sort of right but also a bit wrong. It *is* a book club, but probably not the type you're thinking of."

Intrigued, I lean forward. "Tell me more."

Piper, too, leans toward me, lowering her voice a bit. "Let me ask you this. Have you ever read a book that pulled you in so deep and you related to a character so much that you wished they were a real person?"

I nod. "All the time."

"Have you ever developed a crush on a character? Or wondered what it would be like to have them on *this* side of the pages, if only for a little while?"

I nod again, my eyes sliding to the three book covers I noticed earlier, feeling the blush return.

I remember wishing Aiden, the main character, would step from those pages and into my bedroom and act out everything he did with Lana in that chapter, but with me instead.

"I think we all have." Piper settles back and opens the laptop between us. "So, Haley, that is the basis of what we make happen for our exceptional, carefully selected clients."

Wait. *What?*

My brain considers and then rejects a half-dozen possibilities of what she could mean, and I can see she's waiting for me to absorb her words and come to a conclusion.

What if…?

Nope. That cannot be. That would be like…

I jump off that train of thought before it runs away from me and decide to let her tell me what she's talking about.

"I'm not sure I understand what you mean, Piper."

She laughs, a light tinkling sound. "I think maybe you do, but I'll explain anyway."

"It's not just you. I, and the two ladies that run this with me, realized about a year and a half ago that many women and men feel the same. If you scroll through any of the popular social media apps, they're all about book boyfriends. Who their favorite is, which they don't like, etc. The book fanatics talk about the characters as if they're real people, even though we all know these book boyfriends are a fantasy."

Piper pauses and stares into my eyes. "But what if they weren't? That was the question we wanted to answer. So my partners and I devised a way to bring them to life for those extraordinary clients."

Book boyfriends. Brought to life. It *is* what I imagined.

"How... how does that work, exactly?" I'm intrigued, obviously, but I can't figure out the how part.

Piper grins widely, triumphant. She knows she's got me.

"Before I explain all the ins and outs of the process, I need to know you'll be discrete."

I frown. "Okay, is there like a secret handshake or something?"

Piper lets out a girlish giggle as she slides the laptop closer to herself. "There can be, but our members usually sign an NDA."

A non-disclosure agreement? That sounds serious. Is this real life?

While I sit, slightly shocked but eager to hear more, Piper quickly types something on the laptop, her long nails clicking on the keyboard. When she's done, she spins the laptop around so the screen faces me and hands me a rubber-tipped stylus she pulls from a little drawer on the table.

I scan the screen as swiftly as possible, noting the multiple paragraphs of tiny writing that would take me quite a few minutes and my reading glasses to read. At the bottom, I can make out a line for my signature and date, explaining the stylus.

"What does it say?" I ask, lifting my eyes to hers.

"This form only says that anything you and I discuss today doesn't leave this room. This isn't the membership paperwork. We'll get to that if you decide to move forward."

I don't give myself time to second-guess but instead follow my instinct. With a flourish, I sign my name on the screen as Piper watches.

After all the drama with Ben, I'm ready for a new adventure.

"Here's how it works." Piper stands and moves around the room, gesturing as she speaks.

"The confidentiality works both ways. Whatever you do here is private, between you and your partner. Yes, partner. We don't call them characters or actors; we want you to be completely immersed in your experience. To put it in the simplest of terms, you are a club member, you pay your dues, and you book experiences based on your membership level, much like any other club."

"How many levels of membership are there?" I'm fascinated by what she's saying, and I know it's written across my face.

Piper smiles. "I'm glad you asked that. There are three: Bronze, Silver, and Gold. The Bronze tier is what we call 'dates.' For example, your date experience may be in a movie theater or a fancy restaurant with your partner. It would be a casual, first-date type of scenario. For instance, your date may involve hand holding or end with a kiss on the cheek, depending on the book you've chosen."

That sounds fantastic; I can think of three book characters with whom I'd love to go to dinner or a movie.

But I have to know more. "What's the next tier?"

Piper stops near the table and taps one long finger on the surface.

"First, let me say this: you're in charge of what happens or doesn't. There are no hard and fast rules in any tier. That said, Silver is a lot like Bronze, but enhanced. By that, I mean that your 'date' goes further in terms of intimacy. That is to say, more kissing and petting, you could say. Do you understand what I mean, or should I explain further?"

Wow. Fleetingly, I wonder how this isn't prostitution, but I'm not about to ask Piper that. I'll have to Google the legalities later.

I nod. "I get it. And the Gold tier?" I'm sure I already know the answer, but I ask anyway.

"Full intimacy. It can go as far as it does in whatever book scenario you choose. You are in charge here. These are your fantasy partners. Again, before you ask, our partners have all been vetted with full background checks and medical testing. They've also signed NDAs of their own. Almost all of them have other jobs or careers and want to keep this to themselves. Also, none are in relationships. If, and this has happened in the past, one of our partners does start a relationship, they are let go from the program. We don't hire anyone who's engaged or married, and have a careful process to make sure of it."

Her sympathetic look suggests that she's thinking of what I've just been through with Ben and Sasha.

Funny. I haven't thought of him once since I've been here tonight. That's a good sign, isn't it?

It almost feels like I should be scandalized and leave the room in a huff, but I don't. I'm more intrigued than ever, but I do have more questions.

"How much does it cost?" I ask, my practical nature taking the lead.

"The Bronze level is our most affordable, and the tiers go up from there. I'll give you a menu of services before you leave if you want to take it home and think it over."

Piper comes and sits down, scooting her chair next to mine. She takes my hand and covers it with her other one.

"Haley, I know we've only known each other a little while, but as soon as you came in earlier and told me about what happened with your ex-fiancé, I knew you were right for this. You've hinted at how little experience you had before him, and I feel this is a perfect way for you to explore who you are and what you want." She releases my hand. "So what do you think?"

"I… I think I would like some time to consider it. This is a lot to take in at once."

Another gentle smile. "Of course. Let me get you a few things to take home, okay?"

Chapter 9

Decisions, Decisions

A few minutes later, I'm sitting in my car but I don't start the engine. My mind is reeling with all I've just heard, the possibilities, the consequences.

I don't know if I want to laugh or shake my head or… report this to the police.

Just kidding. I had no idea things like this *smut club* even existed, much less that I'd be invited to one.

I'm dying to look at the brochure Piper gave me, but I'm going to wait until I get home. A shower and some tea should clear my head.

I'm home, freshly showered, and in my favorite pajamas. Grabbing a blanket, I curl up on the sofa with a steaming cup of tea, slip on my readers, and reach for the brochure.

In keeping with the discrete theme, the thin booklet has a matte black cover, pretty scrolled corners, and two pink intertwined hearts in the center.

I open it and start reading. Most of it covers a lot of what Piper's already told me, with some legal jargon and logistics stuff thrown in that she and I didn't discuss. I scan over the paragraphs, noting answers to most of the questions I'd thought about on my way home.

Finally I get to the paragraph I'm most interested in.

I'd been wondering about the "selection" process, and the booklet explains how that works.

Since I already have an online account with the store, once my selected membership is paid and active, a new button will appear on my home screen when I log in to the website.

From there, a new window will open where I'll choose books I'd like to experience a scene from and add them to a special wishlist. I'll pick a date and time, and then Piper and her crew will choose one from my list and set up the scene. Then, I'll receive an email with my official "club meeting" info.

All I have to do is show up, and I guess what happens next will be up to me, right? There will also be a check box for an option to experience multiple scenes from one book.

I put the brochure down and rub my forehead. Am I actually considering doing this?

Yes. I am.

Why not? I'm single and inexperienced. This could be life-changing in all the best ways. And somehow, remembering the other women in the waiting room gives me the courage. They're doing it; why shouldn't I? Based on the way the booklet explains it, there's nothing inherently wrong or illegal happening. So, why am I hesitating?

I pick the pages up again and turn to the last section. Pricing.

I nearly drop my teacup when I read how much each tier costs.

It's expensive. Prohibitively so. I can't afford even the cheapest membership on my teacher's salary.

I feel the familiar pressure and sting of tears rising as I realize I wanted to do this. I wanted to join the club and have book-boyfriend experiences in a safe, controlled environment. I wanted to explore my sexuality and learn who I am, what I like, and what I want in my next partner.

Deflated and more than a little sad, I curl into the sofa and rest my head on my knees for a moment, willing myself not to cry.

When I'm about to get up and dig around in the freezer for a pint of Ben and Jerry's to drown my sorrows in, my phone alerts me to a text.

I sigh as I reach over and check the screen.

Great. It's Ben. Of course, it is.

I almost don't look at it, but that won't make it disappear; he'll keep texting until I answer. So, I swipe to unlock my screen and read the single sentence.

> Mother said to tell you we need the ring back.

In case I wasn't clear before, *Mother* can go f…

Wait a minute.

The ring.

Tossing my phone aside, I fling off the blanket, scramble off the sofa, and sprint down the hall to my bedroom and into my closet.

From the top shelf, I take down my small safe and type in the digits to unlock it, entering the wrong code twice in my excitement.

When I finally get the code right, I open the lid and there, nestled in its small black box, is my engagement ring.

All six karats sparkle back at me—perfect color and clarity.

Appraised at and insured for a hundred and fifteen thousand dollars.

Thank you, Ben. I just figured out how I'm going to afford that membership.

As I leave the jeweler the next morning, I don't feel guilty in the least.

I didn't hate the ring, exactly. It just wasn't my style. It was huge, where I like understated, and it was an ultra-modern design, where I'd have preferred something that looked a bit more vintage.

The appraisal and the insurance policy list me as the ring's owner, so there is no legal trouble there. And morally? Nope. I consider this payment for the lost months of my life.

I leave with a full wallet and a smile on my face. Due to broker's fees, I didn't get the whole amount for the ring, but I got plenty—enough for whatever tier I choose, with a lot left over.

I can't wait to call Piper.

Chapter 10

Pick One

Thankfully, Piper had an opening for a meeting for the next afternoon.

I'm in the secret room with the book covers again, and now that I know what they represent and what awaits me, I see them in a whole new light. They sort of serve as the menu, if you will.

As I wait for Piper to finish up my contract, I look around, wondering how many women are in the club, then trying to guess which book from my list will be my first experience.

Last night and again this morning, I dug through all my books, making a complete mess of my shelves, pulling my favorites, highlighting or tabbing scenes I'd love to experience, and adding them to my private Club wishlist.

At the beginning of this visit, I learned that Piper owns the building next door in addition to this one, and that's where the rooms that have been converted for the club are. I think about how often I've come into this store just to browse and had no clue what was happening just a few walls away.

Once Piper has completed her portion of the paperwork, she leaves the room for a moment to grab a printed copy for me to sign.

I opted for the first tier of membership… at least for now.

When she returns, we review a few points I needed clarified, and then, again, she hands me a pen to sign.

I do so without hesitation.

Piper tucks the papers away in a file folder and we both stand. Are we supposed to shake hands or something? *Was* there a secret handshake?

But no. Piper links her arm with mine and walks us around the room, slowly circling the table.

She gestures to the walls and says…

"Welcome to the Boyfriend Club. Pick one."

Chapter 11

A First Time for Everything

I'm beyond anxious. A little terrified, a lot excited, my emotions are rioting, each fighting for first place.

Tonight is *the* night.

I've chosen my book; now all I have to do is quit being a chicken and get my butt dressed and over there; I can't afford to be late. The booklet said that if you're more than fifteen minutes late for your "date," you have to re-book for a different night.

Even though I picked the "low intimacy" tier, I'm nervous. Soon, I'll be meeting a stranger for an intimate encounter. I try to convince myself that, if I think about it, it's no different than going on a blind date, except that I know what will happen in advance.

After much debate, for my first experience, I picked one of my favorite billionaire romances, *Winner Takes All*. Something about a man in a tuxedo just does it for me.

I'm glad I don't have to worry about an outfit. Piper's "immersive experience" includes costuming, hair, and makeup. I have a particular scene in mind, and if the scene plays out as it does in that chapter, soon I'll be clad in a red satin cocktail dress and dripping diamonds.

I throw on a tee and overalls, slip into flip-flops, and gather my purse, keys, and courage.

Let's do this.

As it has been on my previous visits, the lights in the bookshop are dim, but that doesn't bother me anymore. It's what's waiting inside that's got my stomach in knots.

Again, Piper meets me at the door, and we quietly make our way to the back of the building.

I expect to be led to the door we used before, but Piper surprises me by stopping at the last bookcase on the left. It's an ornately decorated one I've visited many times since it's one of the most popular shelves in the store.

The sign above reads "Hot New Releases," filled with titles I've seen recommended on social media apps.

Right away, I spy a copy of *Winner Takes All,* and the knots in my belly tighten a bit more.

Piper reaches up and pushes the top right corner of the bookcase, and, I kid you not, the entire thing swings inward, just like it would in a children's fairytale.

I look at Piper. "Seriously? A secret bookshelf door? Am I in Wonderland?"

"Go on through, Alice," she replies, laughing.

There is no hallway; instead, the hidden door opens right into what appears to be a dressing room.

It's… impressive, at the very least.

There are half a dozen individual stations, and I step over to the nearest one. There's a wide vanity table with a huge lighted mirror hung above. Dozens of makeup choices are neatly laid out on the vanity top. A selection of jewelry is on hooks to one side of the mirror, and on the other side, an array of wigs in different styles, lengths, and colors is displayed.

At the far end of the room, the wall is lined with racks filled with all sorts of costumes, and there at the end is *the* dress.

The red, satin, floor-length masterpiece looks exactly as I imagined it in my head. Off the shoulder, slinky, side slit to the thigh, I can all but feel how the smooth fabric will slide on and mold to my body because it also appears to be *just my size.*

Glancing over my shoulder, I see Piper leaning on another of the dressing tables, silently watching me.

I tilt my head to the dress. "Is this… ?"

"Yep. That's your dress for tonight. Whatcha' think?"

What do I think? It would be difficult to put words to my feelings right now, so I just ask, "Can I put it on?"

Piper comes over and slips the gown from its hanger, then hands it to me, the cloth cool and smooth in my hands.

"This is your night. Start with the dress, and then we'll do your hair and makeup."

She points to a curtained-off booth in the corner, and we begin my transformation from schoolteacher Haley to Brianna, Ethan's fiancée.

I'm stunned by my reflection in the mirror.

As I guessed, the dress is the exact right size. It shows the perfect amount of cleavage, nips in at the waist, and flares over my hips. The rest cascades in a scarlet waterfall to the floor, stopping right above the matching suede peep-toe pumps I found waiting for me on a little shelf in the dressing room.

As I stand before the full-length mirror, marveling at the fit of the dress, I hear a knock at the main door. I push the curtain aside and step out to see Piper open it, allowing two women to come in. One of them carries a metal case in each hand, and the other wheels in a matching one, suitcase-style. Piper sits in an empty chair nearby as the taller of the two women begins unpacking her tools.

"Haley, this is Sharecia and Maxie, hair and makeup." She gestures to the dark-haired beauty and the leggy blonde, and I wonder if being gorgeous is a requirement for working here.

"They'll style you according to your scene, but you can change anything you want. Remember, this is your experience, and it is completely customizable. Come sit, try to relax, and I'll bring you some champagne. How's that sound?"

I'm reassured by Piper's speech and settle in for my transformation. "It sounds perfect."

Chapter 12

Winner Takes All

A **Scene from "Winner Takes All"**

Some thirty minutes later, I'm feeling a bit more mellow (I blame the champagne).

I've been groomed to within an inch of my life. My hair is in a half-up-do, just as described in the book, and I've got a smoky eye that is so perfect I know I could never recreate it. I have to admit… I look damn good.

Sharecia carefully removes the smock that protects my dress, and I'm ready to go.

Piper leads me out of the dressing area and down yet another hall to a solid-looking wooden door, one of maybe a dozen along this corridor. As we stop in front of the closed door, she takes me by the shoulders and turns me to look at her, giving me a head-to-toe once-over. I guess she likes what she sees because she nods in approval.

"You look exquisite, Haley. Go in whenever you're ready, and remember, you're in the driver's seat. You can take charge or let your partner lead; it's your choice. Do you have any final questions for me?"

"I… don't think so?" It comes out as a question and I press a hand to my belly to calm the butterflies.

Piper pats my arm and steps away, smiling softly. "Go ahead, then."

I turn to face the door, take a deep breath and turn the knob.

It's like stepping into another world, or more precisely, a book scene. The very one I hoped to get.

The spacious bedroom is dominated by a vast four-poster bed in shades of gray and cream. There are two plush chairs on a small rug in front of a fireplace, a marble-topped lady's vanity, and two closed doors across from me. Two bedside lamps and a trio of vanilla-scented pillar candles burning on the mantle softly light the room.

Again, the scene is set up exactly like the scene from *Winner Takes All*. If I remember correctly, and I do, I should sit down on the padded stool before the mirror. So far, so good.

For a few moments, nothing happens. I fidget with my hair, then my dress, adjusting the neckline as doubts creep in.

Why am I doing this? I can find dates on my own without resorting to whatever I'm doing here. Can't I?

As I'm about to get up and leave the room, one of the doors behind me opens, and Ethan steps into the room, footsteps silent on the carpet. I don't turn because I can see him in the mirror as he comes up behind me.

Yes, I know he's not real, but at this moment, I can believe he is. He's got the height, the chocolate hair, and the dark, intense eyes, all just as I imagined him when reading. And he's looking right at me. Holy smokes, my first book boyfriend.

I have no idea what to say or do, but it doesn't matter because he does.

"Hello, darling. I've been waiting for you."

That voice, my god.

It's butter and caramel and chocolate sauce and all delicious melty things. I don't have time to think about that any further because as I hold Ethan's gaze in the mirror, he's moved closer and closer until he's right behind me, and he smells *amazing*.

Where on earth did Piper find this guy? Build-a-Boyfriend? Actually, I guess that's what this is.

In the next second, all thoughts fly from my mind because Ethan has set his hands on my bare shoulders, and all I feel is fire. The warmth of his hands and the flush of my skin combine into a heat I *never* felt with... what was his name again?

Who cares? This perfect specimen of a man is touching me, and our eyes are locked in the mirror as he reaches one hand into his pocket and pulls out... a diamond necklace.

"I brought you something."

He dangles it from one long finger, and it sways gently from side to side. It's one perfect round diamond on a silver chain and despite knowing what's coming, I shiver in anticipation when he unhooks the clasp and lifts the necklace over my head. The stone settles in the hollow above my chest, and as he secures the chain, I can feel his fingers brushing the fine hairs on the back of my neck.

I close my eyes without meaning to. My feelings are so intense that I feel like I may pass out. My heart is racing, and even if Ethan can't see it, I know he's noticed my heaving chest.

"It's perfect. As are you."

I know what's coming, and I hold my breath as a strong hand wraps around my throat, oh so gently, and his thumb brushes the underside of my chin. My eyes are still closed, but I feel his breath on my cheek as he moves closer, and I know what he's going to do next…

I feel so much. I feel *too* much.

My eyes fly open, and I shove away from the vanity, pushing him back in the process. I spin around and see the shock on his face.

"I'm so sorry… I can't.. I have to go." I stutter out my apology, and then, without another word, I run for the door.

As I stumble down the hallway, trying not to step on the long dress, I see Piper approaching me, tablet in hand. I come to an awkward stop, and she reaches out to steady me.

"Haley, what happened?" she asks, concern in her voice. "Are you… hurt?"

I shake my head and feel the first hot tear burn its way down my cheek. "I just can't do this. I don't know what to say, and it was all so much and… I'm so sorry."

Piper folds me into a hug. "Sweetheart, you have nothing to be sorry for. Let's get you changed, okay?"

Chapter 13

Epic Fail

After Piper led me back to the dressing room, she and Sharecia helped me out of the dress and back into my own clothes, neither asking questions nor saying much at all. Once dressed, I assured Piper again that I wasn't hurt, just overwhelmed and needed to go home. She didn't push me; instead, she told me to drive safely and call if I needed her.

Now I'm back at home and feeling stupid, foolish, and immature. Ashamed, embarrassed, even mortified. My teacher's brain is being super helpful in supplying me with words to describe how I feel right now.

In my bathroom, I scrub off the makeup that had been so carefully applied less than an hour before. I allow myself a moment to mourn the perfect smoky eye and then wipe it off with the rest before changing into my pajamas. All that's left is the updo, and I decide to leave it until bedtime.

I intend to curl up on the sofa with the latest Layla Baker. Dark romance is my comfort genre and she's the queen of it.

I'm pacing the kitchen, waiting for my left-over soup to finish warming, when I hear a soft knock at the front door.

As always, I press a button on the security system screen in the hallway to see who it is before going to the door. Single women living alone can't be too careful, you know.

When I see the familiar silhouette standing on my porch, I groan. It's Piper. Due to that whole embarrassing scene at the bookstore, I seriously consider pretending not to be home. Never mind that the lights are on, and my car is parked in the driveway.

Details.

Before I can choose fight or flight, she calls out. "Haley, it's Piper. I know you're in there. Would you open the door, please?"

Well, shit.

Abandoning the plan to ignore her, I shuffle to the door and unlock it. Opening it just wide enough to peek out, I try to apologize again.

"Piper, I am so..."

"Stop that right now!" She interrupts me forcefully. I'm taken aback; I've never heard her raise her voice before, and for some reason, I find it damn funny.

I giggle as I swing the door wide to allow her in. "Yes, ma'am!"

Piper mock glares at me as she steps inside, sets her bag on the table in the entryway, and then points one of those lethal nails at me.

"We're friends, Haley, but if you want to stay that way, never, ever call me 'ma'am' again."

I throw my hands up in surrender. "Yes... um... Piper. Come on in."

Leading the way to the living room, I cast a sad glance at the kitchen, where my soup is no doubt growing cold.

It's not that I'm unhappy to see her exactly; I'd just rather be left alone to wallow in my misery. Not to mention, there's a sharp edge of regret lingering that cuts a little bit deeper each time I remember how I ran out of her store.

We settle into opposite ends of the sofa, and I wait for Piper to speak, to tell me she's disappointed, or, at the very least, to make me explain why I did what I did.

She reads my mind. "I'm not here for an explanation. I just wanted to check on you, as a friend, because we are. You know that, right?"

I feel the waterworks trying to start up again, triggered by her kind words and soft tone. I nod, not trusting my voice not to shake, and sink lower into my corner.

"Haley, what happened earlier… I felt like I needed to talk to you about that, to reassure you, and I thought it was best done in person. That's not the first time one of my clients has gotten overwhelmed in the middle of an experience and had to leave."

It's not? I sit up a little straighter.

"We know the experience can be intense, especially when it's your first time. It's possible that I should have suggested you start a few months from now, considering you're still in mourning for your broken engagement. If that's the case, I should be the one apologizing."

Well, I obviously can't let her take the blame for this, so I rush to correct her. "Piper, I am in no way, shape, or form mourning the loss of Dick, let me assure you."

"Dick? I thought his name was Ben?" she says, puzzled, and again I laugh.

"Ben, I mean. We... my sister and I call him Dick now because... well, for obvious reasons."

My explanation draws a smile from Piper's perfectly painted lips. "Well, that's good to know. At any rate, I feel as though I'm responsible to a degree. I could have waited a while before inviting you to the club."

I scoot closer and lay my hand over one of hers. "This isn't your fault. Ben wasn't a good match for me, and somewhere deep down, I knew it. As far as the rest, that's on me. So I won't call you Ma'am, and you won't blame yourself for tonight. Deal?"

She sets her free hand on top of mine, and we smile. When she releases me, I sit back.

"I guess this is the part where I explain what happened in there?" I somehow feel I owe her this because we are, as she said, friends.

"Sweetie, you can if you want to, or we can talk about something else. Or you can tell me to leave if you'd rather be alone?"

I think for a second, and I realize the company would be nice. I want to talk about my date disaster.

"No, stay. I'd like it if you did. How about some wine?" My stomach rumbles, reminding me of my uneaten dinner, and I have to think fast; I only have one serving of soup. "I've got some cheese and crackers and things, too."

"That sounds lovely. Let me help you." She starts to rise from the sofa, and I wave her back down. "I've got it. Make yourself comfortable, and I'll be right back." I step out and head for the kitchen.

Two glasses of chilled Moscato later, I'm feeling much more relaxed, and the memory of my failed Boyfriend Experience seems a bit fuzzy around the edges. Maybe it wasn't as mortifying as I remember.

Nah. It was the most embarrassing moment of my life.

I smear veggie cream cheese on a cracker and top it with a stuffed olive before shoving the whole thing into my mouth at once. The alcohol seems to have loosened up my care for table manners a bit, too. I glance over at Piper, and she's daintily nibbling on a strawberry.

Brushing the crumbs off my lap and onto the floor, I swallow and wipe my mouth, remembering at the last second to use a napkin and not my sleeve.

"So... " I begin, and Piper waits. "It was all going fine, I thought. My outfit was perfect, hair and nails, and the detail you guys put into it is just... everything. I was trying to remember how Brianna behaved in different scenes of the book so I could do the same and..."

Piper interrupts me. "Sorry, but can I stop you there for a second?"

I shrug. "Sure."

"I feel as though I know what you're already trying to say, and as I mentioned, I've seen this before. Do you remember Charlotte?" I nod, and she continues.

"She had almost the same experience as you her first time, and even though I didn't do a house call for her, this is what I told her. Overthinking the experience is your enemy. You have to let yourself be the character, not someone *playing* the character. Don't think of what Brianna would do; you *are* Brianna. What do you want to do? What do you want to happen? Does that make sense?"

As her words sink in, I slowly nod. "You're saying I need to get out of my head. Right?"

Piper grins. "Basically, yes. The logistics of the experience aren't important. It's our job to worry about that. So, put that part out of your mind. The other thing is, your experience doesn't have to happen just as it does in the books; those are just guidelines, so the team and I can get an idea what kind of things you like. You're free to take the reins and make your date whatever you want it to be. Think of the book scene as a suggestion of what *could* happen."

What she's saying makes perfect sense, and I find… I want to try again, so I say so.

"When can I book another experience?"

Chapter 14

Second Chances

We talk a bit more, and after Piper leaves, I settle back into the sofa and pick up my book, but I don't open it to the marked page right away. My mind is spinning with the possibilities of what Piper suggested. What if I *could* get out of my own way with this, be the character, and lose myself in the experience?

All I know for sure is I want to find out.

Piper asked if I wanted to try the scene from *Winner Takes All* again, but I declined. I'm more comfortable going into something new; I think if I tried that scene again, I'd falter, remembering the earlier failure.

Satisfied with my decision, I open my book and dive back into Layla's world of morally gray men, noting to add this book to my experience list.

Chapter 15

Meant For Me

Scene from "Meant for Me"

I don't know why I'm so nervous. It's not like Kane and I have never had dinner before. I need to get out of my head and pay attention before I break a dish. Kane's a single guy; he doesn't have much in the way of kitchenware.

The lemon-scented dishwater warms my cold hands as I wash the plates we carried from the dining room. The aroma mixes pleasantly with the lavender candles I lit earlier, which still burn on the table.

Our evening meal ritual started a few months ago when I moved in with Kane. He cooks, and I clean. I offered to prepare the meals, too, but he says chopping and stirring relaxes him after a long day at work.

That's fine with me; I can barely boil water, but for Kane, I'd have tried. He saved my life—even if he denies it.

My ex-boyfriend, Chad, and Kane had been best friends since they were little kids, so I've known Kane for about four years now, since Chad and I first got together.

Despite their lifelong friendship, the two men are nothing alike. Kane is a thinker, while Chad is impulsive. Chad is often loud and obnoxious, while Kane has a calm, soothing manner.

More than once over the last few months, Kane's calming influence has kept me grounded when my thoughts threatened to spiral, and I feel indebted to him. I feel a lot of confusing things about Kane these days.

To make a long story short, about a year ago, Chad got fired from his job; the accounting department found evidence that he'd been skimming from the register, to the tune of eighty thousand dollars and change.

I don't want to go into too much detail because that's not what this is about.

Chad's employer agreed not to pursue criminal charges as long as he left the company quietly and made restitution in the form of monthly payments.

Our relationship had been rocky before the incident but got worse after he was caught and had to confess to me what he'd done.

So much worse.

Chad has always been a drinker, but job-less and humiliated, he doubled then tripled his nightly drinks. He grew more and more moody, and then, on the final night, he put his hands on me the way no man should ever touch a woman.

Afterward, he tried to say it was just a push. It wasn't.

Chad shoved me so hard that I flew back and hit a mirror, shattering it, resulting in multiple cuts to my head, back, and shoulders. I hadn't seen it coming, so I had no chance to try to catch myself before impact.

Once he passed out that night, I packed as much as I could carry in a suitcase and a back-pack and quietly snuck out of our apartment into the night.

Except, I had nowhere to go. Chad and I had met online, and I'd moved eight hours away from my friends and family to be with him.

I called Chad's best friend, Kane, the only other person I knew in town.

He took me in and bandaged me up, no questions asked, and shielded me from Chad's texts and phone calls.

For weeks after I moved out of Chad's place, Kane took care of me. He handed me tissues when I cried, helped me move all my things while Chad was at work, and gave me a ride to work when my car's tires were mysteriously slashed late one night.

At first, Chad begged me to come home and give us another chance, but when that didn't work, he made threats and somehow blamed me for what he did. Thankfully, Chad seems to have given up and hasn't bothered either of us for a while now. It's safe to say his and Kane's friendship is over.

As I've said, I've been living here in Kane's apartment for a few months now, and what started as purely platonic has morphed into something new, on my end, at least. I've been trying to deny it, but tonight, something shifted.

If I'm honest, there have been little things I've noticed lately. Kane watches me more and talks to me less. Sometimes he seems on the verge of asking me something and then stops himself before he can force the words out. It's made me anxious around him, and I'm sure he can see it, even if he hasn't mentioned it.

And it's not just him. I'm more aware of his movements, his gestures, his proximity to wherever I am.

Kane looked at me differently this evening as we ate dinner and talked about our day, like always. I told him a joke about something that happened at work, and it made him laugh. As I watched him, I felt some kind of pull; a strong, nearly overwhelming desire to leave my seat at the table and slide into his lap, to hold him and never let go.

"Hey," Kane's voice came from behind me, low and smooth. "Shower's free whenever you're ready. I left you plenty of hot water."

I look back towards the door, and there he is, leaning against the wooden frame, arms crossed over his chest. He's shirtless, clad in nothing but grey sweatpants, fitted in all the right places, and I feel my heartbeat quicken.

I knew when he'd finished his shower. I'd been listening to the sound of the water and daydreaming a bit about how I'd like to join him in there.

He's beautiful, damp from his shower, dark blond hair wet and falling into his face.

"Oh, hey. I didn't hear you come out of the bathroom. Let me just get these last dishes washed and I'll go take mine."

"Let me finish those for you," he said, stepping closer, so close I can feel the warmth of him on my back. "I know you had a long day."

He's always so considerate of me.

I turn slightly so he can see my smile. "I'm almost done. Just these plates left to rinse." I shift again and reach for the faucet handle.

I hate that I have feelings for him; there's no chance Kane will return them. Even though he and Chad are no longer friends, I feel as though Kane would think being with me would be a betrayal of their long history.

"Kylee."

His voice is soft, tender, and close to my ear. I didn't even realize he'd come up behind me.

Kane places his hands on my shoulders, slowly and gently, giving me time to pull away if that's what I want to do. He's always so considerate of my feelings and needs, something I never got from Chad.

I don't want to pull away.

Not right now.

Not ever.

I think… I think I may be in love with him. Maybe I've always been; maybe not. But he's waiting for me to look up at him, and when I do, he asks the question no woman ever wants to hear. Those three words that almost always mean bad news is on the way.

"Can we talk?"

What can he possibly want to discuss? Has he picked up on my feelings? Does he want me to move out?

I could if I had to; I've been saving a lot of my paychecks these last few months because Kane refuses to let me help with rent and bills despite my insistence.

But I don't want to leave. Ever. I want to cling to him and let whatever happens happen. The world could burn down around us for all I care.

Resigned to whatever fate awaits me, I drape the dishtowel over the oven handle and nod.

"Sure. Of course."

Kane leads the way over to the sofa, which is only steps away from the kitchen, not leaving me much time to prepare for this discussion, whatever good or bad may come of it. Regardless, in the few seconds that I walk behind him, multiple scenarios run through my mind: he's going to ask me to leave, or he wants to tell me he has a girlfriend. Or both.

On the sofa, he sits on one end, and I curl up on the other.

"What is it? Did I leave one of my bras lying around again?" There, that came out light and friendly, despite the pounding of my heart.

Kane doesn't crack a smile. He looks serious and a little nervous, maybe.

"So, there's no easy way to say this." I notice he's popping his knuckles, a habit he hates but can't seem to control. "I need to tell you something and I really need you not to freak out."

God. This is going to be bad.

"Please, just say what you need to. Nothing you could say would freak me out."

A generous lie; there are so many things this man could say that would crush me.

In one quick movement, he stands up again and starts pacing the small room, and I can't help but think this must be awful news to have him so agitated, and my anxiety spikes.

"This just might. But I can't keep this to myself anymore, Kylee. I feel sometimes like I'm losing my mind." He glances over at me, his expression almost pleading. "And it's all because of you."

The tension in the room is thick and palpable, like the air before a hurricane.

"Say it." I need this to be over with so I can pick up the pieces of my heart and figure out my next move. "Whatever it is, just say it."

Kane takes one huge step back to my end of the sofa and kneels at my feet.

"Kylee, I love you. I'm *in* love with you." His words come out in a flood, like he's been holding them back by sheer will.

"I don't even know for how long, but if I'm honest, I started having feelings for you when you and Chad were still together."

I stare at him, unable to speak, stunned by disbelief that this is happening, but I want to find the words to tell him… I'm in love with him, too.

I'm saved from having to come up with a response because he isn't finished.

"I've wrestled with this, tried to fight the feelings. I tell myself it can never happen between us; that even though you don't belong to him anymore, you can never belong to me."

But that's where he's wrong.

"I had no idea." I'm dying to touch him but more words need to be said. "Why didn't you tell me?'

Something like hope spreads across his face, and he takes one of my hands.

"Have you never wondered why I never have girls over?"

I have, actually, but I stay quiet. I can't remember the last time I saw him with a woman.

"Have you not noticed that you've been here for months, and not once have I asked you if you've looked for a place to live yet?"

Okay, that's also true.

"That's because I don't want you to leave. Ever. I want you to be mine. Today. Tomorrow. Forever."

"Forever…." I whisper the word because if this is a dream, I don't want to wake up.

He releases my hand and sits back on his heels.

"Listen, I don't want to pressure you—not after everything you've been through—but I need to know. Have I lost my mind? Is there something more between us, more than just friendship? Because I want you to understand I am so grateful for what we have, but do you… is there even the smallest chance of you loving me back?"

As I stare into his eyes, tears rise in mine, and the words won't come. I'm drowning in my feelings, the relief of knowing I can tell him how I feel and how much I've wanted to be his.

My silence has obviously concerned him, and he attempts to change direction. "Kylee, look… I'm sorry. If it's too soon…"

Before he can get the apology out, I press two fingers to his lips. "Shut up."

"Um… okay," he mumbles behind my fingers, and I see the beginning of a smile on his gorgeous face, and that gives me the strength to tell him how I really and truly feel.

"Almost since the day we met, you've been a safe space for me. No one in my life has listened to me or been there for me the way you have. I think… maybe it was always meant to be you and me. Kane… I'm in love with you, too."

With that final word, I launch myself into his arms. We stand still for a moment, with me wrapped around his body, staring into each other's eyes, and then Kane spins us in a circle. Joy spreads across his face, and I know it's mirrored on mine.

Before our lips touch in our very first kiss, he whispers, "You're mind. Kylee, you were meant for me."

Haley, after…

That was amazing! I loved "Meant For Me" so much that I've read it over and over. As a teenager, I had a mad crush on the boy next door, and Kane reminds me of him.

I immediately find Piper and ask if I can do another scene tonight.

Luckily, she had a cancellation. Here I go again!

Chapter 16

Going Down

A *Scene from "Going Down"*

I hate Mondays—especially this one.

I'm late for an interview, my tote bag is overloaded and heavy, and my new shoes are already killing me.

They looked so cute when I tried them on at the store, but I regretted my choice after walking from the parking lot and through the lobby.

Whoever said beauty is pain can kiss my ass.

To top it all off, this elevator is packed and moving at a crawl, and it seems the guy next to me bathed in his overpriced cologne this morning. This set off my allergies, making my throat itch and my eyes water. Rest in peace, perfect winged eyeliner I ever so carefully applied an hour ago.

To be clear, I'm not usually this cranky. But I feel I've earned it.

This latest run of bad luck started when I was suddenly let go from my previous job a few weeks ago. Downsizing, they said. Sure.

Since then, everything has been going wrong. Most recently, I stepped in Miss Sandy's dog's morning deposit on the way to my car today.

I'm desperate to nail this interview, get the job, work my ass off, and turn things around. My bank account, and my pantry, are almost empty.

As I watch the numbers creep higher on the digital board above my head, as I'm sure every- one else is doing, I lean away from Cologne Guy as much as I can without being obvious.

It doesn't help. Everyone in this elevator is *marinating* in the stuff. I try holding my breath, but it only provides a few seconds of relief.

Not only that, but unfortunately Cologne Guy does notice and sends me a death-ray glare.

Great.

Eventually, the elevator reaches the ninth floor, and after what seems like an eternity, the doors slowly slide open.

I'm grateful and relieved that Cologne Guy is the first to step off, taking his stench with him. The rest of the passengers also file out behind him, leaving me alone in the quiet as the doors close behind them.

"About freaking time," I mutter to myself as I kick off my shoes.

At the rate this elevator is going, It'll be another half hour before I get to the twenty-third floor, and there will be plenty of time to get them back on before the doors open again. I flex my toes in relief.

"Great. We got rid of one stink, and now you want to take your shoes off?"

I whip my head around to see to whom the deep voice with the slight southern accent belongs.

Great. I'm not as alone as I thought I was. Out of my peripheral vision, in the back corner of the elevator, is an adorable guy in a suit leaning against the back wall, relaxing as though he hasn't a care in the world, except for his issue with my bare feet, of course.

Embarrassed and irritated, I snap back, "Excuse me. I thought everyone had gotten off." I turn my back on him as I finish the sentence, having decided not to let this man make my day any worse.

Except he seems to have more to say. "Why do you women wear such uncomfortable shoes in the first place?"

You women?

Oh, he's one of *those.*

I close my eyes and silently count to ten, then twenty, just to be safe.

The stranger's accent is adorable, and that makes me hate him. I need to try hard not to unalive this guy before my interview. My ruined eye makeup would be nothing compared to walking in with blood stains on my best dress.

I try a different tactic and a sweeter tone.

Without turning around, I say, "If I promise to put my shoes back on, will you stop talking to me? I'm on my way to an interview and already having a shit day. Literally." I bend down and grab one of my discarded shoes, wiggling my toes once more before I shove them back into their cage.

I hear him take a breath, and I know something snarky is coming my way. But the elevator jolts to a hard stop the next second, the overhead lights flicker, and we're plunged into complete darkness.

I was wrong. The day just got worse.

With one shoe on and one off, I stumble and tip forward, relieved when my hand touches the door and I stay on my feet. When I hear the man curse from somewhere behind me, I pray for the lights to come back on quickly. Being stuck in an elevator with a stranger and his bad attitude was not on today's to-do list.

Plot twist: I'm terrified of the dark.

"Are you okay?" the man asks, again behind me, sounding much closer than before. His tone has changed; he genuinely sounds concerned for me, which, instead of making me feel calmer, heightens my anxiety.

The lights are still off, and I can't see a thing. This guy is creeping closer, and I have no idea what's going to happen next. A thought occurs, and I reach down to feel around in my tote. Somewhere in there, there has got to be something I can use to defend myself.

Wait… my phone. It has a flashlight on it. I abandon the search for a weapon and feel for my phone instead. But it's not in the big inside pocket where I usually stash it. I think back to the last time I saw it, and… *shit.*

My phone, with its handy little flashlight, is at home in my bathroom. I was listening to music on it while I was getting ready this morning, and I'd bet my paycheck (once I get one) that it's still on the counter. Just when I thought things couldn't get worse…

"Um. Hello?" That velvet voice comes from my right side, even closer than before. "I asked if you're okay."

"I… I'm fine," I force out.

I'm not fine. I'm not afraid of many things, but being stuck in absolute darkness is in the top three, second only to Black Widow spiders and knife-wielding clowns. No, seriously, that's a thing.

I sense him shifting around in the darkness somewhere to my right and take two careful steps to the left, my whole body shaking with panic.

"You don't sound fine," he says softly, thankfully a bit further away now. "It's going to be all right; they'll have the lights on any second now, okay?"

My inner child wants to argue, to ask him how he knows that and what if they don't? Are we destined to be stuck here forever?

The adult me doesn't want to admit my phobia to this stranger but does anyway, just to shut him up. "I'm afraid of the dark, okay?"

And what does he do? He laughs. Out loud.

Then there's quiet, with nothing but the sound of our breathing between us.

"Wait. Shit. I'm sorry… You're serious?"

Fear is a powerful emotion, but so is annoyance.

"Yes, I'm *serious*. Not many people know this, but I had a scary experience in the dark when I was a kid, and since then… " I trail off, not wishing to humiliate myself further.

The man doesn't say anything for a long moment, and then I hear, "Hold out your hand."

"I'm sorry but… what?" I reply, bewildered. I just told him one of my deepest secrets and he wants to hold hands?

Again, I somehow *feel* him move closer and then my cold, trembling fingers are sandwiched between his larger, warm ones.

Unbelievably, I feel better when we make this small but essential contact. I can feel the heat radiating from his skin to mine, and I find myself comforted. The tremors all but cease.

"The dark can't hurt you. At least not while I'm around." I can hear the gentleness in his voice, combined with that slow southern drawl, and other parts of me also begin to thaw.

Don't judge; I've been in a dry spell, okay?

Anyway.

We stand together in the pitch dark, holding hands and nothing more. My breathing slows to normal and I guess I'm feeling better about things because I start feeling the pain from my stupid shoes again.

"Ouch. Dammit." This is from me as I try and fail to stretch my toes.

The man gives my hand a light squeeze. "What is it?"

I let out a huge sigh. "It's my feet. They're killing me. And to answer your earlier question... we women wear them because they make us feel pretty, because they elongate our legs, and because they go well with dresses."

A chuckle floats through the dark. "Well, that explains it then. I'll remember that next time I need my legs elongated." I smile as I catch a whiff of his cologne, something woodsy, maybe pine. Not too much of it, just... perfect for him.

This strange but somehow endearing man has managed to relax me a bit and make me smile, which is no small feat considering I'm trapped in a dark, windowless box.

"I guess I should introduce myself, huh? Since we're stuck here, and you're holding my hand and all."

He chuckles again. "What if we don't? Do we need to exchange names? Chances are, we'll never see each other again after today."

I want to argue the point because that's who I am, but he's right. What difference would knowing each other's names make?

"I guess not," I reply, shrugging even though I know he can't see me. "Do you have your phone on you?"

"I don't, why?"

I sigh. "I don't have mine, and a bit of light would be nice right now."

He takes a brief pause and then gently suggests, "Why don't you step back slowly until you reach the wall, and then go ahead and sit down? I'm going to use the emergency call button to check on the status. Sound good?"

Again, I can't find any reason to disagree. "Sure."

When he releases my hand, I leave my bag where it is and move carefully, two steps back, three, and then a fourth. When my palms meet the cool metal wall behind me, I slide down until I'm sitting.

The pressure off my toes is a sweet relief.

I can hear the man moving around in front of me, so I draw my legs under myself so he doesn't trip.

After a few seconds pass, I hear his low curse. "Goddammit. Nothing's working. The power must be out to the whole building."

Oh, no. This can't be. I can't just… stay in here. I lose it.

"You've got to do something! Why don't you have your phone?" I know I'm shouting but I can't help myself; all of the calm from moments earlier is gone.

"Hey," he says, his voice getting closer as he speaks, "You're going to be fine. I promise."

His hand lands on the top of my head and I startle. "What're you doing?"

"Sorry. I was going for your shoulder. Just trying to comfort you."

I don't reply. This whole encounter feels strange and mixed with my phobia, it's all a little surreal.

Seconds later, I feel his shoulder and arm press against mine, and I know he's sitting next to me, back to the same wall. I can feel the warmth emanating from his skin, and I want to move closer, but I know I shouldn't.

"So. Come here often?" he quips. "I'm kidding. Where are you headed, exactly?"

I try to stop thinking about being suspended in a metal cage in the air by nothing but a few cables and focus on his question.

"I have an interview at Ranger, Pierce, and Donaldson this morning, which I'm late for. Now there's no chance I'm going to get that paralegal job. And trust me, I really need it."

After a long pause, he bumps my shoulder with his. "Don't say that. If the whole building *is* out of power, they'll understand. You're technically in the building on time, just delayed a bit."

That does help a bit. It's not like I just blew off the interview altogether. "Hmm. That's true."

As we sit and make small talk, I feel the tension releasing from my shoulders. Surprisingly, instead of frightening, I'm beginning to find the darkness that surrounds us somewhat comforting. There's a certain safety in not being seen but only heard.

After a while, we're quiet, with only the sounds of our breathing between us.

"Hey," I finally whisper, even though we're alone.

"Hey, back," he says, matching my whisper with his own.

"I'd really like to take off my shoes. I can't feel my pinky toes." I hold my breath, waiting to see if he'll mock me again.

He doesn't.

"I can do you one better." I feel him shuffle around and the next time he speaks, I can tell he's moved to sit in front of me. "Give me your foot."

I don't even think about it for reasons I can't explain. I stretch my legs until I feel him grasp one of my ankles, and then my foot is released from the torture device. He takes the other foot and does the same.

"Ow, ow, ow!" I half shout, as the feeling of pins and needles starts in my toes.

"What? What did I do?"

"It's not you; it just hurts when the blood starts flowing again, you know?"

"I know exactly what you mean." I can hear a smile in his voice. "Let me help."

He sets both of my feet in his lap and starts massaging my toes, and I can't help it; I moan.

Out loud.

Another chuckle from the darkness. "That good, huh?"

I can't even be embarrassed. The man is giving my foot some sort of magical massage, toes to heel. Not only are the pins and needles fading, but warm, gentle shocks are running up my legs to my thighs. I shiver involuntarily and let my eyes drift closed, giving in to the sensations. I had no idea a foot rub could be so erotic.

"Cold?" he asks, rubbing the feeling back into my feet with firm but gentle pressure, one toe at a time, giving equal attention to each digit. When he reaches the end of one foot, he starts on the other, pressing his thumb in circles to the sensitive skin of my arches.

"Mmm?" That's all I can manage as a reply. I feel as though my bones are melting under this stranger's touch, and I love it. While not quite what I'd call a sexual encounter, this is for sure an intimate one.

I've almost dozed off, to my utter shock, when he slides his hands up to my bare ankles, squeezing a bit as he goes.

"More?" he asks, his voice low and rough, and it's then that I know what he's doing to my body is affecting him too.

Stupidly, I nod before remembering he can't see me, and I'm grateful for the lack of light that would have betrayed my blush.

"P...please. Yes." I've hardly stuttered out the words, and he's sliding those warm hands up my calves, slowly scraping his short nails along my skin, and I shiver again.

When his hands reach the sensitive skin behind my knee, I can't help myself. I let out a kitten-like mewl at the feeling. Fireworks are shooting off deep inside my stomach, and now, instead of wishing for light, I'm praying we're stuck here together for hours because I never, ever want him to stop touching me.

Just above my knee, his hands still, and I sense he's waiting for my permission to go further. This is the moment, the one where I thank him for a job well done and pull away or let him continue.

I open my mouth to tell him what I want, and the lights flicker once or twice and then stay on. We're frozen, face to face, staring into each other's eyes, and the spell is broken.

He releases me and pushes to his feet as I, flustered as all hell, also ungracefully rise to my feet while attempting to straighten my dress and slip into my shoes.

As reality forces a normal distance between us, I realize what I almost let this stranger do. I know I would have let him go as far as he wanted, and now… now I can't even look at him. We compose ourselves, him way more smoothly than I, and move to separate corners of the elevator.

After a few long, heavy seconds, he breaks the silence. "So..."

"Please don't." I interrupt before he can finish his thought. "Let's just pretend this never happened, okay? I appreciate you comforting me, but the rest... just didn't happen."

I don't turn to look, but I can feel his gaze burning the side of my face. "Okay. Sure. If that's what you want."

"It is," I say firmly, eyes on the doors.

Thankfully, the elevator chooses that moment to continue its journey to the higher floors, moving swiftly upwards as though it was never broken.

At the 23rd floor, we glide to a smooth stop, and I grasp my bag tightly. I'm half thinking of my interview, hoping the partners will still see me, and the other half wondering what the stranger thinks about me and what happened in the elevator.

When the doors open, I step out. Straight across from the elevator, I see a sign showing the way to the office suite for Ranger, Pierce, and Donaldson. It directs me to the first door on the right, and as I turn, I can see the man steps behind me.

"Are you following me?" I stop and turn to face him, impatient to get to the law office and beg for another chance at an interview.

He steps past me and turns the knob to the door.

"No, not at all." His mouth turns up in a half-smile, and he puts his hand out. "I'm Jason, the Pierce in Ranger, Pierce and Donaldson. It's nice to meet you, Alison. I'll be conducting your interview today."

Chapter 17

Not Quite Enough

I'm damn near skipping as I leave the bookshop. I don't stop to talk to Piper on my way out; I want to hug this experience to myself for a bit.

As I drive home, I replay everything that happened in the "elevator."

I'm proud of myself for doing the whole experience this time, for staying in character, for not freaking out or overthinking. I did drive things in a direction a little different from the book, but I'm still happy with how it went. Jason was perfect, and his light southern accent was just how I'd imagined it.

In case you're wondering why I chose that scene... I may have a fantasy that includes my feet. Maybe.

Also, the shoes didn't hurt; that was just part of the book. Piper provides only the best clothes, shoes, sets, and everything else.

And can we just talk about Kane and Kylee? I love that whole friends-to-lovers thing, especially when her ex was such a giant douche. Also, you can't go wrong with grey sweatpants…

Chapter 18

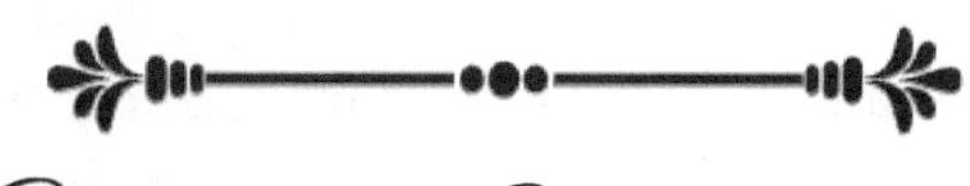

You and Me, Again

A *Scene from "You and Me, Again"*

There's nothing fun about grocery shopping. It's less fun on a Saturday afternoon when the stores are full. It's *even less* of a good time when it's two weeks before Christmas and you're hauling around a cranky baby, bumping into someone every time you take a step this way or that in one of the overcrowded aisles.

I hold a jumbo pack of diapers in my left hand as I juggle Aimee's carrier in my right. As my crap luck would have it, there were no available shopping carts to be found anywhere near the entrance.

I seriously consider abandoning this trip and returning later, but I'm out of everything: milk, bread, eggs, and, most importantly, we're running dangerously low on diapers.

Not for the first time, I think how much easier this would all be if Aimee had a father. Of course, she has one; I just don't know who he is.

Believe me, I know how that sounds, but hear me out. Before that one time, I spent my whole life being the mature and dependable one in my family.

The one time in my life I stopped being responsible, I had a one-night stand, and my daughter, Aimee, was the result.

I haven't had another one or any kind of relationship since then. All my time and energy has been spent keeping this tiny human safe, happy, and healthy.

As I try to add a packet of wet wipes to my already fully loaded arms, Aimee wakes up and starts fussing for a bottle, a clean diaper, or both.

I know from experience that the fussing will turn into a full-blown fit in less than thirty seconds. I've got to get out of here before that happens and we cause a scene.

I quickly decide most of the food items aren't necessary right this minute; I'll take the diapers and wipes and return early tomorrow for the groceries. Jiggling the carrier a bit to soothe her,

I look down at Aimee as I round the corner into the bread aisle, eyes scanning for the quickest route to the checkout area.

And then— *Crash*.

I hit a solid wall of manly chest and stumble back a few steps, almost dropping the diapers, wipes, *and* carrier. When I manage to hang on to both items and my child, I look up to apologize to whomever I just rudely barreled into.

But the words won't come. It's him.

The man I'd spent that one perfect night with. The one who gave me my daughter.

We hadn't exchanged names, numbers, or promises. We were just two people who wanted and needed each other, just for a few hours.

When his eyes meet mine, I see the spark of recognition, and trying not to panic, I say something profound.

"Hey."

The man smiles back and starts to respond in kind, but then his gaze drops to Aimee's carrier, and several expressions cross his face in quick succession, which is just as handsome as I remember. There's confusion, then understanding, and then… disbelief.

He stops and starts a few times, struggling to choose what emotion to address first.

"You're… Are you… Is she… ?"

The answer to all three is yes, but I'm frozen, unsure what to do next. I never thought I'd see him again; the hotel room we shared for those short, blissful hours is about three hours away from where I live.

I have no words for the situation I find myself in and no idea what to say or how to explain.

I didn't know where to find him or where even to start. I'd spent days driving around that town after I found out I was pregnant, hoping to see him out somewhere and dreading what he'd say if I did come across him. After each trip, I came home empty-handed, and finally, overwhelmed with what lay ahead of me, I gave up.

"Yes. I am, and she is." I meet his eyes, then follow his gaze as it drops down to Aimee, guilt twisting in my gut.

"I didn't know how to find you," I say quietly, the words sounding false as I say them out loud.

Should I have tried harder? Did I do everything I could to track him down?

"She's beautiful. Perfect." He mutters the words quietly, but it is as though everyone around us has disappeared. "What's her name?"

"Aimee. Her name is Aimee Rose. She really is perfect. She's… everything."

"Aimee Rose… That's beautiful." The sound of my… I mean, *our* daughter's name on his lips does something to my heart, and once again, I feel the pull to this man that I felt the night we met—something magnetic, something inevitable.

"Thank you. It was my grandmother's. Aimee means 'beloved'. Um… What's your name?" I ask, feeling foolish that I didn't get at least that one piece of vital information during our night together.

"I'm Liam," he says, his eyes never leaving Aimee. "And you are… ?"

"Shannon." I raise my shoulders to show my full hands. "I'd shake your hand, but… we're probably a little past that, huh?" He has seen me naked, after all.

He rewards me with a slight grin. "Just a little. Here let me help." He reaches out and takes the diaper and wipes, allowing me to hold the carrier with both hands.

Then Liam's smile fades. There's a long silence between us, the noise of the store again fading into the background, the other shoppers going unnoticed.

It strikes me how drastically my life has changed in the last two minutes. I've spent months raising Aimee alone, not knowing what I was supposed to do. Thanks to a diaper emergency, here we are, her father and I, together again.

Liam steps forward, his free hand slightly outstretched, as though he wants to touch his daughter, who has fallen asleep again, completely unaware of how her life, too, is about to be different. His voice has thickened and is rough and emotional when he speaks.

"Look, Shannon… I want to be part of her life. I want to be part of yours, too, If you'll let me. Tell me what I need to do." I can see the honesty in his face, the openness, which was one of the things that drew me to him that one night. In a crowd of strangers, his was the only one that caught my eye.

My heart swells at his declaration but I've learned to be cautious. I have to be. For Aimee. What if this doesn't work out?

"I don't know, Liam," I say. "If I'm honest, I've thought about you every day since that night. Not just because of Aimee but because of how I felt when we were together. But I've made a life for her, and I don't know how to add you to it. It's not as simple as you make it sound."

Liam's face softens.

"It can be, Shannon," he replies, determination in his voice. "I'll do whatever you want. Your rules, your decisions, your pace. Let me be around the two of you, and we'll see how it goes."

Should I trust what he's saying? After all, he's basically a stranger.

My heart twists in my chest. The thing is, he doesn't feel like one. The memory of our night together has lived in my heart and mind for almost two years now, and there's something in the way Liam's looking at me, at Aimee. My instinct tells me to let him in, give it a try, and give us a chance.

"Okay," I say, my voice breaking with unshed tears. "We can take it slow. For her. For us."

He nods, his eyes soft. "Thank you, Shannon. I'm not sure what this will look like, but I want it. You won't regret it, I swear this to you, and her."

I nod and take the first step toward our life together, the three of us.

"Okay. You and me, again. Well, Liam, would you like to hold your daughter?"

Chapter 19

A Bad Goodbye

It's late. I know I should drag my butt back to my hotel room, but my fifteen-year high school reunion after-party is just kicking off. I've been laughing and sharing memories with my old classmates and their spouses and partners, and it feels fantastic.

After leaving the convention room, we moved the party to this bar, but I'm not familiar with the place. It opened in my hometown some years after I left for college. I like the vibe, though, and the DJ is excellent. I've got a good buzz going, and I'm just not ready to let go.

After a rough breakup a few months ago, I've been mostly a hermit at home, nursing my hurt feelings, not anxious to get back out there and be around people.

But this reunion was precisely what the doctor ordered. For the first time in months, I dressed up and did full makeup and hair, and I'm feeling kind of amazing.

It would all be perfect if the creep perched on the next stool would stop trying to buy me a drink.

First, I already have a drink right in front of me, and second, I don't accept drinks from strangers. I don't know many other ways to say "no" without hurting his feelings, so I'm grateful when my old friend Megan comes up and launches us both into a memory of a junior-year prom dress wardrobe malfunction.

We're throwing memories of that night back and forth, laughing until our bellies hurt, when she asks the question I'd been hoping to escape the night without being asked.

"Whatever happened to Kellan?" The minute his name leaves her mouth, the laughter on my lips dies.

I'd been low-key watching the door for him all night. Kellan, my first love. My boyfriend for all four years of high school. The boy I thought I'd marry.

Megan must see how the smile falls from my face and hurries to apologize, laying her hand on my shoulder. "Shit, sweetie, I'm sorry. I wasn't thinking."

I wave off her apology. "No, no. It's fine. It's not like I can't hear his name or anything. It's been fifteen years!" I try to be lighthearted, but I can see the sympathy on her face, and just like that, I'm done with tonight.

In my heart of hearts, I know the main reason I made the trip here was to see him. Sure, seeing some of my friends was nice, but I probably would have been fine with skipping the whole thing. But Kellan never showed up; not to the reunion and not here at the after-party.

Suddenly, I find myself wishing I hadn't come at all. I make my excuses to Megan and offer a quick hug and a promise to call her soon. Once she's left, I gather my bag and slide off the stool to head for the exit.

I feel a bit lightheaded as I push open the door leading to the hall where the elevators are located.

My fingers are not quite working as they should, so I fumble in my bag for my room key. I shouldn't have had so many drinks at the bar, and my eyes struggle to focus as I search my purse pockets.

"Need some help?" a raspy voice asks from behind me, and I whirl around to see who it is. Great—the guy who wouldn't take no for an answer.

"You seem to be having a bit of trouble there." He smirks, and something about the way he's leering at me makes my stomach turn. I glance around, but the hallway is deserted.

"Again, no, thank you. I'm fine. My friend is about to join me."

It's a lie, and we both know it. There's no one around at all.

He grins again, showing a mouthful of yellow teeth, and my stomach cramps painfully. Those drinks must have been stronger than I thought.

I try to turn to run back to the bar, but he grabs my wrist with a dirty hand, squeezing hard.

"Why are you so unfriendly to me, huh? I saw you inside with your little friend. You seemed to like her just fine. Do you not like men or something?"

He tugs me close, and I can smell his breath, which is a disgusting mix of unbrushed teeth and stale whiskey. I gag as I struggle to pull away, but I'm no match for him; he's got at least fifty pounds and eight inches on me.

My head is pounding, and everything in my peripheral is blurred, and now I'm wondering if he didn't spike my drink.

"Let me go!" I shout, praying someone will hear and come to my rescue.

Now would be a good time to remember what we learned in that self-defense class at work a few months ago, but I'm finding it nearly impossible to focus on anything as sick as I feel; only self-preservation instincts are holding me upright.

There is one thing I clearly remember from that class: go for the genitals. Except he's sort of to the side of me, so there's no clear shot. I stop struggling and let my arm go limp.

"Sir, please let me go. I don't feel well." I allow him to turn my body so that we face each other.

"That was the point, sweetheart. Now be good and hand over your purse and phone," he replies. It's then that I know for certain I was right about the drink. I have only one chance to get away from him, and I take it while he's still gloating.

I raise my right knee and shove it as hard as I can up between his legs, and thankfully, it's a bullseye. Down he goes, curling up on the carpet, clutching his man bits and moaning.

And then I run. Or at least I *try*.

I make it no more than two steps before I slam into a hard chest, and now it's me who cries out.

He brought a friend.

I fight with everything I have left, which isn't much, flailing about while the man who's now holding my arms is trying to say something, comforting words that sound like "You're okay, I've got you," and something… something about his voice makes me stop struggling and raise my eyes to his face.

I see a pair of chocolate brown eyes I know as well as I know my own. I blink once, then again, but he's still there.

Kellan.

The man writhing on the floor behind me is forgotten as I stare into the face of my ex-best friend, the love of my young life, the one who got away.

His eyebrows come down to a point before he whispers, "Jess?"

Just like that, the heartbreak and years between us disappear, and nothing matters—not how scared I was moments before, not how he broke my heart so many years ago, nothing. In this moment, it's just him and me and everything we were together, everything we'd meant to each other.

Memories rush back: late summer nights, swimming in my parents' pool, our first time together in the basement of his house, and… the day he brought everything crashing down. The day he told me we shouldn't go to the same college, and then, as a final crushing blow, he told me he wanted to see other people.

Kellan is still looking at me expectantly, and I realize I haven't yet said a word to him.

"Um, hi." Another wave of nausea passes over me, and I sag against him. "Can you get me out of here, please?"

Kellan looks over my shoulder at the man who attacked me, who's by now struggled to his feet and is trying to limp away as fast as he can. His mouth is set in a hard line, and I can tell, knowing him as well as I do, that he's trying to stay in control of his emotions.

"Did he hurt you?"

"No… not really. He wanted to rob me, demanded my purse and phone. At least, I hope that's all. I think he put something in my drink, though. I need to lie down."

Kellan guides me to a bench behind us and helps me sit down. "Stay here."

Calmer now, I hold up my head with one hand and watch him stalk towards the man. The guy hasn't made it far; I did a good bit of damage there.

The good news is that I'm starting to feel normal again between sitting and gulping fresh air. At least good enough to notice how well Kellan fills out his slacks.

The last fifteen years have been good to him.

It doesn't take long for Kellan to reach the guy, and with one quick move, he pulls the guy's hands behind his back, whips a pair of handcuffs from a pouch hooked to his belt, and snaps them on the creep's wrists. One hard shove and the guy hits the floor again, landing flat on his ass, and I swear I hear something crack.

"Don't move, " he orders, then pulls a cell phone from his pocket. He dials, waits a beat, and then speaks to someone on the other end. "This is Detective Starnes. I need a unit at The Crowne Hotel, sixty-six forty Main."

Detective?

He listens for a moment and then responds in short, clipped sentences. "Simple assault, at the least. Probably aggravated sexual assault. Yep.

In her drink. Good. No worries, he isn't going anywhere. Thanks."

He ends the call and glares down at the creep, who also has his head in his hands and… is he crying? Yep.

Just then, a security officer walks past the end of the hall, doing a double take when he sees Kellan, me, and the sobbing man.

"Hey, come down here a minute," Kellan calls out, and the security guard obeys. I watch rapt as this boy-turned-man barks orders. "Stay here with this guy, would you? One of my officers will be over shortly to get him."

Without waiting for a response, Kellan turns and comes back to me in four long strides. He crouches down, laying a hand on my shoulder, and I shiver. "Cold?" he asks, his brown eyes full of concern.

"A little," I lie. It's not the temperature that has me trembling; it's him. His nearness is having the same effect on me it always did, even though years and years have passed, a fact my body seems to be unaware of.

"Do you have a room here?" I nod. " Okay, good. Let's go. How are you feeling?"

He gently pulls me to my feet and leads me a few yards down to the elevator, where I push the button for my floor.

"Much better. If that guy did slip me something, I must not have had much." It's true; I'm feeling almost normal again.

Once we reach my room and are safely inside, Kellan goes to the mini-bar and grabs a water bottle. Twisting off the top, he takes a drink and hands it to me.

"See if you can drink this; it should help." I take it gratefully. I hadn't realized how parched I was. The nausea recedes with every sip.

Again, his nearness is intoxicating. As we stand a few feet apart, we stay quiet for a long moment.

The silence feels awkward, so I try to fill it. "So, how long has it been?"

"Fifteen years, four months, and eleven days," Kellan replies without hesitation.

Holy shit. He knows exactly how long it's been, down to the day. And what is that I hear in his voice? Sadness? Regret?

It can't be. The breakup was Kellan's idea. I know I'm not remembering that wrong; it was a defining moment at that time of my life.

"Wow," I manage. "That's precise." I laugh lightly, trying to make a joke, but he remains quiet. "Anyway, it's… nice to see you. You look, well, great."

He turns to me and tilts his head slightly, looking me over. I swear I can feel his gaze touch my eyes, cheeks, and lips.

"You do, too, Jess. Really good." He runs a hand over his jaw, and I love the way he's got a hint of a five o'clock shadow. That's new, and it suits him. He sort of looks the same; he's still the boy I loved, but he's also better. Everything about him is more defined, more manly, more… finished.

"Thanks." I brush my hair back to have something to do with my hands. "I, um, didn't think you were coming tonight."

He grins, making his dimples flash. "So, you were watching for me?" he teases, making me laugh. Again, I see a glimpse of the kids we once were.

I have to quit thinking about what was and focus on now, so I change the subject. "Detective, huh? That's kind of awesome. How'd you end up as a police officer? What happened to vet school?"

Kellan had wanted to be a veterinarian since we were little kids. That dream became our end. Two weeks before we were supposed to pack up and move into our respective dorms at LSU, Kellan came to my house and dropped a bomb. He told me he'd found a better vet program closer to home and wouldn't be coming to New York with me.

It was hard to hear that we wouldn't be at the same school, but before I could tell him we'd figure it out, that we'd see each other on holidays and breaks, he delivered another, much more devastating blow.

Unable to look me in the eye, he mumbled some crap about how he had been thinking about it and decided that since we would be so far apart, it would be a good idea for us to try dating other people while we were at college.

With those words, my world imploded. Since we'd gone from being best friends to being together as a couple, all we'd talked about was how we'd be at college together, and then once we graduated, we'd get great jobs, get married, and live happily ever after.

In an instant, all those dreams were crushed into dust.

No matter how much I begged him to make it make sense, he wouldn't. All he'd say was that it was "for the best." Finally, crying and broken, I kicked him out of my parents' home, screaming through my tears that I never wanted to see him again. Until the day I left for college, I refused to answer the door or the phone, no matter how many times he tried.

And then I left for college. I never saw or spoke to him again.

Until now.

Kellan's been watching me quietly as I took that painful trip down memory lane.

"I didn't go." He looks over and sighs heavily. "I think maybe I owe you an explanation. If you want to hear it, of course."

Do I? I think so.

I walk over to the bed, perch on its edge, and slip off my shoes. Then, fully clothed, I slide under the covers and pat the empty space beside me.

"I do."

He walks closer but stops a foot or so short of the bed. "Are you sure? We can do this another time. I know you must be exhausted."

I point to the bed again. "Come. Sit by me. I want to talk. I promise you I'm feeling better."

His eyes search mine, looking for a lie. Seeing none, he sighs and sits beside me, almost as far away as possible.

It doesn't matter. We're together again after so many years, and I'm grateful to have this time with him, as long or short as it may be. Maybe I'll even get some closure. For so long, I've wondered where we went wrong, if I'd done something to drive him away without realizing it.

Once he's settled in, I turn on my side, stuffing a pillow under my face. "I'm ready. Talk to me."

He's so quiet at first that I worry he's changed his mind, but then he speaks without looking at me.

"First, I want to tell you it was all my fault. I did what I thought was right at the time."

That's all he gets out before I interrupt. "How could it have been right? We were meant to be together. That's what we always said, remember?"

"I do. Listen, Jess. This is hard for me, so let me just tell it my way, okay?"

I reluctantly agree. "Fine." I want to hear him out; it's just that I have so many questions.

He chuckles and there are those dimples that made me fall for him when I was just a kid.

"Still stubborn, I see. Anyway, when I told you I found another school closer to home, that was a lie. When I said that I thought it would be best if we saw other people, that was also a lie. "

Mind reeling from this revelation, I forgot I was supposed to stay quiet. "I don't understand, why would you…?"

"Jess, *please*." The pain I can hear in his voice shuts me up. "I'd gone to your house to tell you that, because of some financial stuff that had come up with Mom and Dad, I'd be going to school closer to home. I knew it would be hard on both of us, but I wanted to make it work. I knew we could survive the distance and separation, that our bond was strong enough. But when I got there, you weren't home. You'd run to the store for your dad. He let me in, and I told him what was going on."

He stops and takes a huge breath. "This is the hard part."

He looks so tortured that I reach out and take his hand, tucking it between my cheek and the pillow. It's nearly automatic; we used to lie like this when we were kids, when I'd sneak him into my room after my parents had gone to sleep for the night.

He smiles a little, probably remembering it, too.

"Jess, I never wanted you to know this, but being here with you now, it's almost like fate wants me to tell you the whole truth. Your dad…. your father asked me to break up with you."

I sit up, stunned, releasing his hand. "He did what?!" This cannot be true. I'd know. Wouldn't I?

"Don't be angry with him. He said he wanted to ask me, man-to-man, to do something for him. He said your real life was about to start, and he wanted you to experience everything possible. That he'd worked his whole life to pay for your college and wanted you to find yourself. And that you couldn't do that if you had me hanging on to you. When he put it like that, and knowing that I couldn't go to school with you… at the time, it made sense. And I agreed."

I don't want to believe it, but I know my father, and truthfully, I can see him doing this. I can picture him saying the words in that way of his, that for a moment, you believe everything he says is truth.

"I'll think about that later. But tell me, why didn't you come for me afterward? It's been fifteen years!"

"Because, Jess. You hated me for what I did. And as time passed, what your dad had asked made sense. We're from a small town. I heard about you, about your college years, your top-of-class graduation. Assuming you'd moved on, I didn't want to mess with any of that."

My heart breaks again, just as it did so many years ago, if not more. I can't help it. I cry. I cry for the young girl whose romantic dreams were smashed; I cry for the lost years we could have had together.

I cry because I loved the boy, and I know I still love the man he is now. This is why I've had a string of failed short-term relationships. It's the reason I've never married. There's no one I ever wanted to tie myself to except Kellan.

I've decided that at some point, I'll think about it and try to understand my father's motives. But not right now. Because I'm not going to waste another minute being away from Kellan.

Kellan is watching my face, reading my emotions as he always did and like no one's done since.

"What are you thinking?'" He looks nervous and sad, and I want to touch him again, but first, I have some questions.

I settle back into the pillows, calmer now. "Are you married?"

He seems taken aback by the question. "No, never been."

That's a good start. "A girlfriend?"

I see the beginning of a smile on his face. "Not unless my dog, Macy, counts."

Hope blooms. "So, you're single. Unattached." Now, it's a statement, not a question.

He scoots closer. "Yes to both."

I feel the broken pieces of my heart trying to weave back together as I take him by the shirt and tug his face to mine.

"I've missed you every minute of every day for fifteen years."

Kellan threads his hands into the hair behind my head and pulls me closer, slowly, inch by inch.

"Jess. Me, too. Would you consider giving me another chance? Maybe forever this time?"

I barely manage to nod before his mouth takes mine, hot and urgent, as though he's been a man starved for all these years, a feeling I understand all too well. I'm nearly frantic, trying to touch as much of his skin as I can, as quickly as I can, and he's doing the same.

As we kiss, we whisper love words, old and new promises. Soon, our bodies press together, familiar but also new.

After over a decade apart, we've found each other again, and I'm never, ever letting go. Starting tonight.

Chapter 20

Just a Little More...

That. Was. Spectacular.

Who doesn't love a good second-chance romance?

Still… I'm thinking of taking this a little further…

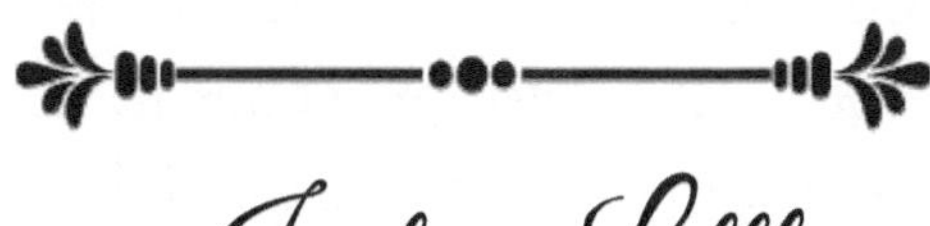

I spend the rest of the night sorting my books into three piles based on their spice level: closed door, light spice, and mostly smut. All my annotation supplies, markers, sticky notes, and highlighters are lined up on the coffee table, ready to help me mark my favorite scenes to add to my Wishlist. I pull my hair into a quick bun and get to work.

When I run out of books from my personal collection, I log onto Facebook and scroll to my favorite book group. I joined The Bookish Retreat group a few years back, and I've gotten so many amazing book recs from the members that I know I'll get a ton of ideas.

By the time I've finished writing down all the books my friends in the group recommend, I've added almost two dozen more books to my Club Wishlist.

That should be enough.

For now.

Chapter 21

The Mechanics of Love

A *Scene from "The Mechanics of Love"*

I open the heavy metal door and startle at the loud screech it makes. Way to welcome your customers. A little oil could help with that.

It doesn't really matter; the rock music blaring through the garage speakers drowns out the sound beyond the doorframe. I step further into the shop, taking in my surroundings.

The inside of the motorcycle repair shop is surprisingly clean. The mechanics' bays are neat and orderly, the tool racks lining the walls are organized, everything is in its marked place, and the floor is swept. I haven't been in many places like this, but it's far from what I thought I'd be walking into.

At first, I think I'm alone so I wander down one row, my sandals silent on the polished concrete floor. A quick glance at my watch tells me it's just after two in the afternoon, way past lunchtime, which makes me wonder where everyone is.

There's no use calling out; the music would cover any sound I made, so I make my way to the back wall, where I see two glass-walled offices, the large windows again sparkling clean. It's clear that someone really puts a lot of care into this place.

When I get close to the first door, I raise my hand to knock, but before I make con-tact with the wood, someone taps me on the shoulder. Surprised, I stumble and lose my balance. A tanned, tattooed arm wraps around my waist, keeping me upright. I try to catch my breath, which isn't easy, considering my back is pressed up against what feels like a rock-hard chest.

Regretfully, I pry the arm away from my middle and turn to see who it belongs to.

Wow, is all I can think.

My savior is tall, at least six-four, towering over my much smaller frame, and I have to crane my neck to look up at him.

His short beard and thick head of hair are both a gorgeous mix of ebony and platinum, and his sleeveless shirt not only fits like a glove, showing off his muscular chest and abs but also showcases the full tattoo sleeves running down both arms. There's a chain wrapping around the right arm with what looks like a pocket watch hanging from it; the other arm sports a religious medal. The ink is spectacular, clearly done by a true artist.

When I manage to tear my eyes away from his arms and meet his gaze, I can see by the twinkle in his near-black eyes and the half-smirk on his full lips that I amuse him, and for some reason, I find it annoying.

"What's so funny?" I demand, but my words disappear like smoke into the chords of the Disturbed song blaring from the speaker over our heads.

Now, the smirk is a full-blown grin, and despite myself, I'm also amused.

The man reaches into the pocket of his work pants, pulls out a tiny black remote, points it at the stereo system resting on a cabinet a few feet away, and abruptly stops the song.

As we stand there staring at each other, I find I miss the distraction of the music. Now, all I can hear is the pounding of my heart, and I pray to whoever that he can't hear it.

"Nothing. Nothing at all. So… can I help you?" he asks, his voice low and husky.

All the ways he could *help* me bounce around like ping pong balls in my mind, preventing me from forming a coherent answer to the question.

Another moment passes, and his eyebrows draw together in confusion as he waves a big hand in front of my face. "Hello? Anyone home?"

I blink and stutter, "I think so…yes. I'm here to pick up some parts. I mean, they're for my brother. He's working late and can't make it before you close. So he asked me to pick them up." I'm rambling but can't seem to stop. "He said he was going to text the shop owner and let them know… but I guess he didn't."

Smooth, aren't I?

His dark eyes sweep me from head to toe before he responds. "You're Jolie? Sean's sister?"

The sound of my name coming out of that mouth…

"Um, yes. So if you could just get him for me? The owner?"

I wonder why everything I say sounds like I'm asking his permission.

Hmmm. I can imagine another scenario that involves me asking for permission...

I shake myself back to the present and notice his hand is out. Confused, I glance down at it and then back up to his face. "What?'

"See, it works like this. I put my hand out, and you shake it. That's how civilized people introduce themselves."

As he helpfully explains the mechanics of a handshake, he extends his left hand, takes my right, and puts it inside the one he still has out-stretched.

His palm is warm and dry, and his huge hand swallows my small one. He doesn't shake; he holds on, and yep, the mythical *electric shock* I've always heard about does indeed run from his hand to mine.

"I'm Rhett. The owner. The guy you... came for." The corner of his mouth lifts in a sly grin.

My breath catches in my throat at the double entendre. I caught his underhanded meaning, and I can tell he knows I did. Lord, help me. I'm about to turn into a puddle at this man's feet.

Regretfully, I pull away the hand that's still captured in his and take a healthy step back. Unfortunately, there's nowhere to go as we've somehow backed up to the wall next to the closed office door. Before I can move sideways to put a bit of distance between us, he takes one giant step forward and places his hands on either side of my head, flattening his palms on the wall beside me.

"Excuse you. What are you doing?" I meant to be firm, but I sound like a scared little girl, my breath caught in my throat, threatening to choke me.

He ignores my question.

"Are you married? Or otherwise with someone?" he asks instead, his eyes burning into mine as though he's trying to search out my deepest secrets. The way I feel right now, he can have them.

I'm not, and even if I was, I have a feeling I'd be regretting it right about now.

"Not at the moment." I shake my head. "I mean, no, I'm not." The air around us is charged with a tension I've never felt before, and I'm simultaneously terrified and excited about what may happen next.

"Thank God," is his only response. A split second later, his mouth is on mine, somehow firm and insistent. As my lips part in surprise, he takes advantage and slips his tongue into my mouth, searching and tasting, and then back out, nipping my bottom lip with his teeth.

Soon, way too soon, he pulls his face from mine and slides his hands down the wall. With a single step back, he lets me out of the cage I'm no longer sure I want to be released from. I miss his nearness as soon as he moves away, and the air between us cools my burning face as I struggle to find my composure.

I should be shocked. I am a little.

I should be scandalized. Instead, I'm aroused.

I should be angry, slap his face, call him names. I'm not, and I don't.

I want him to do it again, so… there's only one thing to do.

"Will you do that again… please?"

I watch, rapt, as a range of emotions flickers across his strong features. First, surprise, then calculation, then finally landing somewhere around satisfaction.

"Will I do that again, please… what?" He crosses his arms and spreads his feet slightly apart, adopting a dominant stance, as he waits to see if I'm really saying what he thinks I am.

I tremble, knowing I'm hurtling to the edge of this cliff without a parachute, but I throw caution to the wind and jump.

"Please… Sir."

With a sound I can only describe as a growl, Rhett reaches out and wraps his hand around the back of my neck, yanking me towards him before scooping me up, strong hands around my waist. I wrap both legs around his hips, and with a curse I can't quite make out, he takes my mouth again, deeper and more roughly than before. He's holding me up with one arm around my back and the other under my ass as he kisses me like I've never been kissed before. It's possessive, as though I belong to him and only him, and I return the favor, matching his pace and letting him do as he likes.

It seems to go on for an eternity, and when he breaks the kiss, I feel lost and confused. I find myself grateful that he's holding me up because there's no way I could stand on my own two legs after *that*. Sparks fly from my skin everywhere he's touching, and I don't know why he can't see them.

The next thing that comes out of his mouth sends a rush of heat flooding through my body.

"Good girl."

With those two words, I'm lost. I know nothing of this man except his name, but I'm ready to give myself to him, body and soul.

Deep down, I know this is madness, and I have to regain some control of the situation.

Pulling in a few deep breaths, I push away from his chest, unwrapping my legs until I'm standing on my own again. I wipe my mouth with the back of my hand and send him a dirty look.

"Don't play the injured party with me, baby girl. You were in it just as much as I was."

I hate that he's right. I hate that he made me lose control. I hate how much I love how he just called me Baby Girl.

My hair is mussed, so I reach up and try to smooth it while thinking about what to say or do next. I've never had a reaction like this, such a quick attraction to a stranger, never acted with such reckless abandon. I'm serious, I'm steady, I'm dependable, but this man... This man is *magical.*

Hair in place, I straighten my shoulders and face him. "You're right. I don't know what came over me. I'm sorry."

His look is incredulous. "What the f... You're sorry?"

His voice is like thunder, and for a moment, I'm afraid of what he might do. I didn't mean to offend him, but clearly, I have, and again, I wonder if anyone else will be returning to the shop soon.

I'm lying to myself; his attitude is a turn on.

Rhett grabs my wrist and roughly pulls me towards a corner of the shop where a massive, gleaming motorcycle sits in an empty bay. I stumble a little trying to keep up with his long stride, but he makes no attempt to slow down.

As we draw near, he points to a spot on the floor. "Stand there. Don't move."

I obey. What else can I do?

He stalks around to the other side of the enormous machine, and I watch him swing one long leg over the bike and settle into the seat. He fits on it as though it was made for him, and my heartbeat accelerates again as he extends a hand to me once more.

"Come." That's all he says. I hesitate to take his hand, unsure of what's happening. Are we going for a ride? Do I need a helmet?

There's that cliff again. I step closer and move to take his hand, but he grabs me by the waist again, lifts me into the air as though I weigh nothing, and sets me on the seat in front of him. Backwards. Facing him.

I'm tucked into his front, my legs thrown over his thighs, and he slips his hand under my knees and pulls me closer until there's no space left between us.

Rhett leans into me, closer and closer, until I feel his breath brush my cheek. "Hold onto me," he murmurs into my ear. I put both hands on his waist, confused about how this will work. He plants his feet and tilts the bike so it's no longer resting on the kickstand but straightened out, upright on its wheels, as if ready to take off.

When he's got the beast steady, he reaches a long arm around my back to touch something I can't see. The bike roars to life, making me jump. The powerful engine breaks the quiet of the garage and rattles the walls with its thunder-like growl.

I don't get it. Why would... *Oh.*

My unspoken question is forgotten as the vibrations of the massive engine beneath me send tiny waves of pleasure through my lower body, rendering me speechless once again. Rhett's hands grip my thighs, holding me in place, pressing me down, as I try to wiggle away from the pressure building stronger until the waves are intense, overwhelming, and threatening to drown me, a fate I'd willingly accept.

He says nothing but silently gazes at my face, my parted lips, my half-closed eyes, watching, watching… until all at once I come apart, gasping and trembling in his arms, calling his name as I slowly come down from the heavens.

"Rhett!"

"Such a good girl. Get ready for another."

Chapter 22

Where Scenes Come True

Wow.

Who knew being someone else for a little while could feel so satisfying and…. sinful?

Even though I'd stopped short of the highest tier, I feel as though I now know what I like and want. The elevator scene in *Going Down* showed me what turns me on, then the hotel scene in *A Bad Goodbye* was way hotter, but then… Rhett and the bike garage.

Kink unlocked.

I know the rules. You cannot go 'real life' with the Boyfriends or exchange real names or phone numbers. Yeah, yeah, okay.

But I admit I'm curious. Why do these men do this? All the boyfriends I've had experiences with were gorgeous. Obviously, that's a job requirement, so it's not like they're ugly to look at. Each of them stayed in character the whole scene, but of course, they've been doing this much longer than I have.

The bottom line is this: Piper and her band of merry matchmakers are freaking geniuses to come up with something this brilliant. The club allows you to do anything, be anyone.

I mean, who hasn't closed a book after a chapter and thought, "If only he were real…"? I know I've had that exact thought dozens, if not hundreds, of times.

Book boyfriends take you out of your reality, whatever it may be, and drop you into your perfect relationship for however long it takes you to finish that book.

The Boyfriend Club and Piper, quite literally, make scenes come true.

Chapter 23

My Mind's Made Up

After much thought, I decided not to graduate to the third tier.

In fact, I'm taking a break from the Boyfriend Club. It's not an issue for Piper; you can pause your membership anytime, and for however long you'd like.

Don't misunderstand; I love being a member. But something happened with Rhett; something inside me shifted into place; I felt a "click" when I was with him. It's hard to explain because even though I know he's just a random guy getting paid very well to play a book character, I know now that's what I want in a real-life relationship. Someone older, someone who takes charge. Someone who makes me weak and wet and wanting with a single look. Everything I *didn't* have with Ben.

I want someone with whom I can share my secrets and whose burdens I can help carry. Someone I know, in a room full of people, is always, *always* looking around for me.

It feels strange that I go days without even considering Ben. Not very long ago, I was ready to walk down that overdecorated aisle and become his wife.

I guess everything happens for a reason; thanks, Sasha.

So, what's everyone's favorite dating app?

Chapter 24

Everybody's Doing It

I t's Saturday, and I'm waiting for Lindsey and Ellie to arrive for girls' night. Of course, there will be snacks, sweets, and wine, and after we've shared a bottle or two, they'll help me get dressed up and take photos for my dating profile.

I decided on *Matchmaker.com,* which is supposedly the latest big thing in dating apps. Lindsey's been using it for a few weeks and has already had two promising dates.

I haven't told her or Ellie about the Boyfriend Club, but I know I'll at least let Lindsey in on it one day. I've never been comfortable keeping secrets from my sister.

I'm piping the buttercream icing (canned, not from scratch) on the last batch of double chocolate cupcakes I baked earlier when I hear a knock at the door.

"Come on in," I call out so I don't have to put my icing bag down, knowing she'll hear me.

The front door opens, ushering in my sister, who enters with a flurry of activity. She's juggling a huge tray that I hope holds those cute finger sandwiches I love so much, a smaller tray with her famous seven-layer taco dip, and two huge shopping bags. I have no idea what's in the paper sacks, but I do know Lin, so it's bound to be something fun.

"You should have texted me from the car; I'd have come out to help," I admonish as I slide my baking things to the side to make room for her to set down her packages.

Once her arms are free, Lindsey steps over and gives me a huge bear hug from behind. "It's fine. Ellie pulled in behind me, and she's bringing in the rest."

"The rest?"

"Yep. She may have brought her whole make-up collection for the photoshoot tonight."

I wouldn't doubt it. Ellie, while naturally gorgeous, is a magician with cosmetics, and there's no way I won't look amazing once she's done with me.

"I'm too full to get dressed," I moan from the corner of the sofa. "Let's play dress up another day."

Without lifting my head, I survey the sad remnants of our feast laid out on the coffee table.

"Agreed. I don't think I can move from this spot." Lindsey lies on the rug, eyes closed, seeming half asleep.

All the taco dip is gone, we've put away two dozen of those tiny sandwiches, and we each had two cupcakes, not to mention the two empty wine bottles at my feet. At this rate, I won't fit in any of the outfits I found in Lin's bags.

"You bitches better get up right now!" Using the tone I'd only heard when her daughter was misbehaving, Ellie kicked my leg, and damn it, it *hurt.* "I didn't drag all this crap over here to watch the two of you take a nap. Go wash your face and pull your hair up. We're doing this thing."

Groaning, I struggled to sit up and do as I'd been told. "Fine. But if I look like a wildebeest, it's on you."

Some forty-ish minutes later, I do not look any-thing like a wildebeest. By the way, none of us knew what one was or looked like, so we had to Google it.

Did you know that wildebeests belong to the antelope family?

Anyway, I don't look half bad. Lindsey picked my outfit: a pair of boyfriend jeans (fitting, I think), a cute black tank, and a cropped denim jacket. We left my hair down in loose curls and finished it all off with a smoky eye and natural lips.

I look like me, but *better*. Ellie is a miracle worker.

This outfit says "Haley" so much more than the hated lace dress of wedding rehearsals past, and, not for the first time, I feel a rush of gratitude for being out of that situation. Also, being a member of the Club boosted my confidence enough that I feel ready to go out and meet people. Even if I don't fall in love right away, at least I know what I want and *don't* want.

No spoiled brats. No momma's boys. No trust fund babies.

Which probably cuts my prospects in half, but we'll see.

Chapter 25

Oh, Hell no.

Sixteen drafts later, I settled on a bio for Ma tchmaker.com.

The screen name was Lindsey's idea; feel free to blame her for it.

BookwormBabe985, female, 26

I want to connect with someone kind and honest who loves quiet mornings and cozy nights, movie and dinner dates, and weekend road trips. I don't have any kids, but I would like to meet someone who would consider having them one day. Not looking to play games or for one-night stands.

Surprisingly, matches started rolling in within the first half hour of me creating and activating the profile.

I took screenshots of the most outrageous ones to share with Ellie and Lindsey at our next girls' night.

Do you want to see a few of them? Yeah? Okay, but consider yourself warned.

BabyDaddy1994, male, 30 – 20 miles away

I'll just put it out there: I'm looking to procreate. You gotta be knocked up within the first six months of dating. If you don't like this, don't waste my time. HMU if you're ready to be my BabyMama (see what I did there?). Oh yeah, I need to see pics before we chat. Only unfiltered pics will be considered.

Oh, Hell no.

ShotCaller$$$, male, 28 – 39 miles away

I own three cars and two homes and have seven fat bank accounts. I need my woman to be at least this successful, if not more. If you can match this energy, hit that message button ;) By the way, I have a strict weight limit on candidates. If you have to ask what it is, you're probably over it. Let's not waste each other's time, k?

It sounds like he's broke and homeless—hard pass.

__Ur1andonly, male, 33 – 28 miles away__
Things I won't do: Cuddle, "Good morning" text, listen to you whine about your job/friends/feelings, or meet your parents.
Things I will do: Tap that azz.

Things *I* won't do: Swipe on him. This guy makes Ben look like a catch. (Almost.)

__TheBigOne23, male, 30 – 44 miles away__
Let me be honest: All men are liars. If you're interested in one who lies __less__ than most, I'm your guy. Swipe, and let's see what happens. PS. Only financially independent females need to apply.

I have no words for this one.

__SometimesFootballFan, male, 31 – 16 miles away__
I can't dance, but I can cook. I love dogs but am allergic to cats. I enjoy staying home or going on adventures, your choice. My toxic trait is thinking my "dad jokes" are funny. (They aren't.) My best trait is that I'm 6' tall so reaching things off the high shelves for you is not a problem. If any of this sounds interesting, send me a like.

Hm. Maybe there's something here…

After much internal debate, two root beers, and a party-sized bag of Fritos, I decide to swipe right on "Sometimes" for a few reasons. His photo didn't appear to be filtered or overly staged, so that was a mark in the plus column. I also love dogs, but not cats, and I can't dance either.

As my finger hovers over the screen, I realize three-quarters of my brain and other body parts are still obsessing over my date with "Rhett," but I know there's no point, and I need to get over it.

Putting that thought out of my mind as best I can, I swipe the red bar from left to right. What have I got to lose?

Chapter 26

Surprise, Surprise

To my surprise, Sometimes (who we can now call Keegan) messaged me about twenty minutes after I swiped him.

After we got through the icebreakers (name, age, occupation, etc.), the conversation flowed well.

Keegan is an underwater welder, which sounds dangerous but also very cool, so we chatted about how he got into the field. Then, I told him I'm a schoolteacher, which he thinks is cute. He has a Cavalier King Charles Spaniel named Joey, never skips family dinner with his parents on Sundays, likes kids but doesn't have any, and is nearly as obsessed with late-nineties music as I am.

I relayed all this to Lindsey and Ellie in a group text, and we all agreed that he sounded promising.

After a week and a half of messaging exclusively through the app, we officially exchanged phone numbers, and Keegan invited me out on a first date.

Excited but still wary of online dating, I say yes when he asks to take me to The Oak House, a fancy new steakhouse one town over. And he's already offered to treat me, which is nice. I was stressing a bit over what to do when the bill came, not knowing if I should pay, or if he does… Ben had a credit card. His mother's, of course.

Anyway, wish me luck.

I check my phone for the third time. I'm more than twenty minutes early. Seated inside the restaurant's waiting area on a plush leather chair, I glance around while trying not to be too obvious.

This place is *nice*. Stained concrete floors, cushy chairs, and white-over-black linen tablecloths create a cozy but elegant atmosphere.

Low music and glass chandeliers complete the high-end feel of the place. And the *waitstaff*. Everyone is young and good-looking, and I feel a bit self-conscious. It's like something out of one of my books in here.

My phone buzzes in my sweaty palm and I check it to find a message from Lin.

> Um, helloooooo. Did you make it? Please tell me this guy didn't chop you into little pieces and stuff you in his trunk.

> Yes, Mom. Safe and sound. Also, what is *wrong* with you???

> Don't act like it couldn't happen, you never know about people. Like, what kind of name is Keegan? It sounds made up. I bet he played soccer in high school. No wait. He was a wrestler!

I chuckle and tuck my phone away without replying. Looking back up, I notice a man who's got to be my date, standing near the door, staring at me. I'm relieved to see that he looks exactly like his photos.

Ellie told me that it's common for men on dating apps to not only use filtered photos but also post pictures of themselves from years and years ago. Thankfully, it seems Keegan has done neither.

I stand and offer a smile.

Keegan is probably the six-foot he said in his bio, taller than me, but not so much that I'd have to crane my neck to look up. There's enough height difference that I feel comfortable wearing these heels. He grins back, his even white teeth gleaming in the dim lighting of the waiting area.

"You must be Haley," he says, offering a hand, his voice deep and smooth, reminding me, *again*, of Rhett.

I've got to stop thinking of a man who didn't really exist at all. He probably wasn't even as impressive as I remember.

Maybe.

"I am. You're Keegan." I put my hand in his and it's dry and warm. "Nice to meet you."

He squeezes my hand and then releases it, and I'm grateful he didn't try to come in for a hug. I'm not a fan of that kind of intimate gesture when first meeting anyone, much less a strange man from a dating app.

"And you also. I want to say that you look just like your photos. That's a nice surprise, " he says, gesturing to the hostess stand so we can check in for our reservation.

"It's like you read my mind." I wait as he gives her his name, and she gathers two sets of wrapped silverware from below her station. When she asks us to follow her, he lets me go ahead of him, which I find considerate.

From behind me, he asks, "What do you mean?"

I throw a playful grin over my shoulder. "The same thing you do. I was pleased to see your pro-file picture is current and not one from 2012," I joke, earning a laugh.

Once we're seated and waiting for a server to bring our menus, we pick up the conversation again.

"Does that happen to you a lot? Men not matching up to their photos?" Keegan asks as he pours me a glass of ice water from the frosty pitcher on the table. Again, very gentlemanly. I wish I could text Lindsey an update, but it'd be rude to pull out my phone, and so far, this is going well.

Taking a slow sip, I consider carefully before answering. "Actually… this is my first date from the app. Have you been on a lot of them?"

I wonder, if he *has* done this first date thing multiple times, if it would be rude to ask why none of them worked out.

Keegan looks uncomfortable momentarily and then replies, "No, not really. Just a few."

As his words fade, a silence that quickly moves towards awkwardness settles over the table, so I decide to jump in and save the conversation.

"So, do you come here often?"

Someone shoot me. That sounded cheesy, and I want to hide my blush behind my napkin.

Luckily, it has the desired effect, and he chuckles. "No, this is my first time, but I've read a lot of good reviews."

"I've seen that, too," I say, as I open and then begin reading the menu he helpfully hands across the table. "Everything looks great."

A more comfortable silence descends as we peruse our menus, commenting on items we may try and deciding on an appetizer to share.

Once our selections are made, we set the menus aside and quickly pick up the conversation.

"Okay, Haley. How about this? Tell me one random thing about yourself that not many people know."

That sounds like something straight out of a first-date-how-to manual.

"I have to ask; where in the heck did you come up with that question?" I smile to let him know I'm just having fun with him.

The tips of his ears redden and he looks down at the table. "I may or may not have Googled 'first date conversation starters' while sitting in the parking lot. Is that terrible?"

It's not terrible; I think it's adorable, and I tell him so. "Not at all," I say, batting my lashes a bit, hoping I look flirtatious and not ridiculous.

There's a fifty-fifty chance.

For about fifteen minutes, we manage to make light and fun conversation without any weird pauses.

Our appetizer arrives, a duo of mushroom crostini and bacon-wrapped shrimp. Keegan considerately lets me choose first, then he fills his plate. I take note of his table manners; that's a big thing for me.

He lays his napkin on his lap, uses a knife and fork instead of his hands, and chews with his mouth closed. All green flags in my book.

I'm about to compliment him when he glances up and startles at something behind me.

Before I can turn to see what's surprised him, an angry female voice sounds behind me at a volume dangerously close to a screech.

"Keegan, you freaking snake. When you said 'out of town for work' what you really meant was 'out to dinner with some slut"?"

Chapter 27

Not Again

My first thought was *Slut? Me?*

Closely followed by *this cannot be happening to me again.*

As I turn toward the voice, I can already feel my stomach churning, and I'm glad I haven't eaten anything yet.

A red-eyed, messy-haired blonde woman stands behind me, majorly underdressed for the venue in her joggers, sports bra, and floppy sweater. More importantly, she's staring down at me (the aforementioned slut) with murder in her eyes.

"Look, I…" That's all I manage to say before she interrupts, pointing one long, manicured finger right into my face.

"Shut up, slut. I'm talking to my husband."

Slut, again? This crazy woman needs to broaden her vocabulary, but also…. excuse me? *Husband?*

It seems as though this *is* happening to me. Again.

Floored, I shut my mouth and turn back to see how Keegan, the *married* guy, is taking all this.

Not well, it seems. He's turned tomato red, and the veins in his neck are bulging above his collar, to the point I'm concerned he's having a stroke. Actually, no, I hope he is having a stroke, which will paralyze him all the way down to his… never mind.

He's alternately staring at his wife, then at me, then back to her again, but not saying anything. To move this along, I'm considering throwing my glass of ice water in his face when he finally speaks.

"Grace… I… It's…" As she did me, Grace interrupts.

"You what? It's what, exactly? I am so interested in hearing your explanation for this. Well? Out with it!"

I risk a surreptitious glance around the restaurant and notice about ninety percent of the other patrons have stopped talking and eating and are staring this way, also eager to hear his explanation. Before I turn back to what's happening at my table, I see more than a few phones being pulled out, likely to record and share this momentous event.

"So. Um. Well, do you remember a few weeks ago, when we were in bed, and I asked if you'd ever consider bringing in a third, and you said you'd think about it?"

Oh, no, he did not just say that.

"Oh my God, Keegan. That was pillow talk! Not permission for you to go out and find us a girlfriend! What is this, like an interview?!" Her voice has risen a couple dozen octaves so far, with no apparent end in sight.

"Well, I didn't know!" shouts Keegan, who is also now on his feet. "And anyway, you're the one still talking to your high school boyfriend! Didn't he dump you for that hot blonde?"

Nice deflection there, dude.

"Are you talking about *Randy*? He messaged me exactly once, and I told you about it when it happened! This is so not the same thing, Keegan!"

Keegan no longer resembles the charming guy who pulled out my chair just minutes ago; instead, he looks like a kid caught cheating on a test.

By this time, the two of them are going at it at top volume, and from the corner of my eye, I can see two heavily built men in dark suits and ties striding purposely between the tables towards ours. We've caught the attention of security.

I've got to get out of here. As calmly as possible, I gather my purse and jacket and step away from the table without a word to either of them.

They don't notice.

I let the tears fall once I'm safely alone in my car. Resting my head on the steering wheel, I allow myself a few moments of self-pity. I'm usually pretty calm in stressful situations, but this is the worst.

What is it about me that gets me this sort of treatment from men? Ben wanted me, but also, not only me. And now this guy, who I should have known was too good to be true, only wanted to "interview" me to be some plaything slash unicorn for him and his wife.

As I sit in my darkened car, raindrops start to fall on the roof above my head, and a memory comes to mind. When I was a little girl, my mother and I would sit together in her rocking chair on the porch during rain storms, lulled by rain tapping on the metal porch roof. I remember those moments as some of the most peaceful of my young life. Right now, I feel like my mom is sending me a message.

"Okay, Momma. I hear you." I dry my tears on my sleeve and start the car. "No more feeling sorry for myself."

Before pulling away, I shoot off a text to my sister.

So… He's married.

I beg your finest goddamn pardon?

Yep. Can you come over?

Already putting my shoes on. Open a bottle, I'll bring snacks.

Chapter 28

One Way or Another

The way I see it, I have two choices. Well, maybe three.

One, I can resume my membership to the Boyfriend Club. I really enjoyed it, and I still have credits I can use. In the last few weeks, I've read a ton of new books I could see doing scenes from. My only concern is that as much as I liked all three dates, the only one I *loved* was with Rhett. What if no experience measures up, and I leave unsatisfied?

Or, I could try the online dating thing again. I mean, one bad date doesn't mean I should give up completely, right?

However, I've been reading dating app experience threads on Reddit, and it seems that there are more scammers and shady characters on the apps than genuine men looking for real connections.

At the end of the day, that's what I want. If I'm going to date, it's going to be with intention, with an endgame of, if not marriage, then at least a long-term relationship. I don't want to settle for anything less.

If neither of those happens, I could give up the Club and the apps and wait for a man to fall into my lap.

Yeah, okay.

What I need right now is to talk to my sister. I need her advice, and that means... It's time I told her about the Club.

"Wait. Just back up a damn minute."

I watch from the sofa as Lindsey paces my living room, her face set in hard lines, brows drawn to a point. "How could you not tell me about this? We're not just sisters, remember? I'm supposed to be your best friend!"

Shit. I've hurt her. That's the last thing I meant to do.

"You are! Honey, I'm so sorry," I apologize, wanting to wipe that look off her face. "I know you're mad, but…"

"Mad?" My sister stops pacing and whirls to face me. "I'm not mad, I'm freaking jealous! We could have spent so much time looking through the books, helping each other make scene choices, and most importantly… dishing after the dates!"

She throws a hand to her forehead, leaning back dramatically, "Oh, the agony of missed opportunities!"

And with her return to humor, I know we're okay. Also, she's right. It would have been fun to do all of those things with her. Deep down, I was worried that she'd judge me, and I was wrong for it. I should have known better.

Done with her over-the-top reaction, she comes back to sit with me, picking up her discarded wine glass and taking a healthy sip.

"So," she starts, grinning at me over the rim, "Tell me everything."

I'm far from shocked when Lindsey expresses her desire to join the Club, but we both know she can't afford it. I don't mention it to her but I have enough cash left over from the ring fund to buy her a membership, so I consider that a gift for her upcoming birthday.

I tell her everything that happened on the horror fest of a date with Keegan and his wife, and by the end, I'm able to laugh at the ridiculousness of the whole thing. Once the wine and snacks are gone, she asks if I want her to spend the night.

"I'd love that, honestly."

"Done."

Later, after we've changed into our pajamas and settled into my bed, my sister asks for a bedtime story, just as she did when we were kids.

"Sure. What'll it be? Princesses? Dragons?" I ask, rearranging my pillows into a comfortable pile to lean up against. I send her a sideways look. "Please don't say unicorns."

We both giggle. Once we've gotten our laughter under control, she says, "First, I have a question."

I roll my eyes without looking her way. Of course, she does. "What is it?"

"Hypothetically... For research purposes, of course... How would a person apply for a job at the Club?"

She bumps my shoulder with hers, and I turn to her in time to catch her sly grin. "I'd like to be the person who interviews the actors, or whatever you call them…"

"Lindsey Marie!" I kick my little sister under the blanket, even though I've also considered that very same thing. Talk about loving what you do for work…

She winks at me. "Just kidding. Mostly. Anyway, tell me again about Rhett."

Chapter 29

I Remember You

Six weeks, five days, and two hours later…

Until recently, I've never really understood what people meant when they said they were "taking time to work on themselves," but that's what I've been doing.

I've put my club membership on hold indefinitely. It's not that I think I won't ever use it again, but something is holding me back that I can't quite put my finger on. Also, I've muted the two dating apps I was on, as I can't handle another Keegan anytime soon.

For now, I'm doing as the cliche says, focusing on me.

Part of my new self-care routine is going on bi-weekly dinner dates to my favorite sushi restaurant. Sometimes, I invite Lin or Ellie, but most of the time, I take my Kindle, pick a table somewhere in the back, and stuff my face with fish, crab, rice, and seaweed while enjoying some people-watching between bites.

I love the duality of being in public places alone, with people but separate from them. Something about the hushed conversations and gentle clink of silverware soothes me, especially after a long day of teaching a dozen rambunctious kids—bless their little hearts.

Tonight is one of those nights. Tucked into a rear table near the hall leading to the kitchen, I mix my soy sauce and wasabi in a little bowl for dipping and dig into the Crunchy Crab Roll the waiter just dropped off at my table.

Kindle ignored, for now, I admire the curve of the waiter's butt as he walks away. Without looking down, I swirl my first piece of roll in my sauce and pop it into my mouth, a decision I immediately regret as fire rivaling the seventh circle of hell hits my tongue.

I added way too much wasabi, and I'm on fire. My nose instantly starts running, my eyes burn, and I gasp for breath as I blindly feel around, looking for my water glass to quench this heat.

I feel a warm hand touch my back lightly.

"Hey… you okay?" a deep, concerned voice asks from somewhere to my left as I finally wrap my fingers around my glass. Ignoring the tinge of amusement I heard from whoever asked the question, I drink greedily until the glass is empty, thankful when I'm somewhat able to breathe again.

Once I feel like I may survive this, I glance up at the good Samaritan and start to thank him, even though my voice is more of a wheeze at this point.

"Yes, I'm fine. Thank … " I stop, words lost as I stare into Rhett's eyes. Yes. *Rhett.* From the Boyfriend Club. The man I've been obsessing over day and night for months.

Oh, please, God, no. Anyone but him.

My prayers go unanswered as we stare at each other without speaking. My joy at seeing him again is all but obliterated by the knowledge that my eyes are still streaming and I cannot imagine the state of my makeup, but I'm sure it's on the far opposite side of attractive.

I want to disappear and briefly consider dropping to my knees and hiding under the nearly-floor-length tablecloth until he goes away.

Also, I have no idea where to find my dignity, and that seems like a good place to start looking for it.

Rhett breaks eye contact as he sees a busboy coming towards us and gestures for the younger man to stop. The kid looks terrified, as he's only about five feet tall, probably wondering what this huge, scary-looking guy wants from him.

"Hey, bud, I need you to bring another glass of ice water over here real quick." Rhett pins the poor kid with a semi-glare. "And real quick means right now."

Despite it all, I feel a little overprotective of the skinny, pimply kid, who can't be much over eighteen years old, and I say so, watching as he scurries away with only a nod to do Rhett's bidding.

"You know, you could have asked him nicely, with the same result," I say smartly, half-forgetting what's important here.

It's him.

Towering over me, it's Rhett. The dream man from my favorite age-gap romance, looking just as edible as I remember. Yes, I know that's probably not his real name. Whatever.

Side note: The tattoos are real. Lord, help me. I'm internally combusting for a whole different reason.

"Probably, but that was way more satisfying." He smirks down at me, all smoldering eyes and dark stubble that I immediately want to run my fingers over.

The boy returns to hand me a fresh glass of ice water, saving me from having to articulate a response. But he's gone before I can thank him. Poor kid.

Anyway, this is awkward. I'm dying to know if Rhett remembers me, and I feel stupid for even thinking about it. I'm sure he's had hundreds of women who are way more memorable than me doing scenes with him at the Club, so how could I possibly expect him to remember me?

Come to think of it, maybe it's better if he doesn't. I can introduce myself, pretend I've never seen him before, strike up a conversation, maybe get his number...

It sounds like as good a plan as any, and that's a good thing because it's all I have.

As I consider the best way to implement my plan, Rhett pulls out the chair next to me. I slide mine back a few inches to accommodate his long, long legs. Now, we're practically knee-to-knee.

"So, I really appreciate you checking on me. I was looking at… um. Never mind. I wasn't paying attention and put too much wasabi on that bite. Anyway, you are? Because, honestly, it was so nice of you to… "

I stop my rambling mid-sentence. Mortified at my lack of cool, I drop my head.

Neither of us says a word for a few tension-filled seconds, and then I feel his fingers under my jaw, his thumb on my chin, as he gently, but somehow also firmly, lifts my face to his. His thick thumb brushes the bottom edge of my lower lip and I can't stop, nor hide, the little shiver that runs through me, neck to belly.

I raise my eyes to meet his, and he whispers, "I remember you."

Chapter 30

Boy Meets Girl, Again.

He remembers me.

As he says those three words, everything around us seems to blur, the sounds of the restaurant muted, the other patrons all but forgotten.

Unbelievably, I feel like I'm living inside a romance book scene here and now, but a million times better. This encounter is more intense than anything I could have imagined, more than anything I've ever read.

Rhett (or whoever he is) is leaning towards me, our faces only inches apart. We're close enough that I can see the slight dimple in his bottom lip, and it's all I can do not to reach up and find out how it would feel under my fingertip.

"You… you do?"

He smiles, all white teeth against tan skin, looking like nothing so much as a modern-day pirate.

"Yes. You were my Jolie."

Right now, I'd be his anything. His everything, if he'd let me.

I wish I could tell you the next thing I do is lean in and kiss him passionately but… that's not what happens.

Sadly, *tragically*, I do what I always do when I'm nervous.

"Oh, well, okay. I mean, yeah, that's possible. Did you know the human brain can store roughly the equivalent of two and a half million gigabytes of digital memory?"

He blinks, and the spell is broken. Rhett leans back in his chair and rubs his hand across his chin, tilting his head slightly to the left.

"Well, no. I didn't know that, but thanks, I guess." He's wearing a slight grin, so maybe there's hope of saving this moment.

God, just kill me now. This evening isn't going anything like I'd predicted; it's better in one way but terrible in all others.

Suddenly, I'm exhausted and want to go home and wallow in my misery and humiliation. I lean over and gather my purse and Kindle from the other side of the table, my arm brushing his for a moment.

"I need to go," I say, not meeting his eyes, feeling the start of hot tears in my own. "Thanks again for… the water."

As I rise from my seat and turn to leave, Rhett reaches out and grabs my wrist.

"Wait."

That one word is all it takes to make me obey because my deepest, darkest desire is to be this man's "good girl" in real life.

It's why he's the first thing I think of in the morning and the last at night. It's why I never really put the time and effort into the dating apps. It's really why I stopped using my Boyfriend Club membership.

In him, I've found what I want, and nothing I'd had before or would find afterward would ever, ever match up.

And now, by some miracle, he's here, and he's got my wrist firmly in his grasp. When I turn to look back up at him, what I see in his eyes is anything but fake.

It's a look of interest, of intrigue, the way he looked at me when we did the "Mechanics" scene, but this is no fictional scene. There's a flicker of something else, too, something that looks almost like hunger.

My pulse quickens even further, but not from shame. I feel something like… hope.

I am so wrapped up in what I'm feeling that, at first, I don't catch what he's just said.

"Oh. I'm sorry, what?" I hate the way I sound, my voice trembling with… what? Nerves? Anticipation? *Need?*

Rhett repeats himself patiently but with a hint of a smile. "I want you to give me your number."

A demand, not a request, and I shiver again.

My instinctual answer is that he can have anything he wants, but I stop short of saying so.

"Of course," I breathe as he unlocks his phone and hands it to me, already knowing I'm going to agree.

"Just type it in," he says, watching as I punch in the digits. "Wait… what's your name?"

"It's Haley."

I'm rewarded with a full-blown grin, "Nice to meet you, Haley. I'm Eli."

Chapter 31

Happily Ever

I'm in the middle of drying my hair after a shower when the first text comes through. Hearing my phone chime from the bedroom, I drop my towel and run to grab it, not caring that I'm naked and dripping water everywhere.

Hi, it's Eli. Did you make it home safely? I wish you'd let me drive you.

I did. It's sweet of you to ask. Maybe next time you can take me home. ;)

I regret that one as soon as I hit send. I shouldn't presume he would want to see me again, but then again, he did ask for my number first. I hurry to change the subject before he can respond.

> I was surprised to see you, you know. Do you live near the restaurant?

> Actually, no. I'm probably a twenty-minute drive from there. One of my guys got engaged, and I took him and his fiancee out to celebrate.

> What do you mean, your guy?

> Well, I really am a motorcycle mechanic, and I do own a garage. I have six guys that work for me. That's one of the reasons Piper picked me to play Rhett.

I've been both dreading and looking forward to this. I want to know how Rhett, sorry, *Eli*, got into working at the Club and all that, but at the same time, something pinches in my chest when I picture him with other women.

Crazy, I know.

> I don't want to overstep, I'm not sure what the rules are here, but

is it okay to ask how you got into that? Playing a character in the Club, I mean.

It's a long story, but the shorter version is that my brother dated Piper for a few years a long time ago, and a while back, she and I ran into each other. She told me about a character in this book that I reminded her of and then let me in on what was happening in those back rooms. So anyway, she said I was perfect for the part, and it sounded intriguing. I wasn't in a relationship at the time, so... here we are.

At the time?

Does that mean he's in one now? Wait, no. Piper said none of the "partners" are in relationships. I guess it wouldn't hurt to ask. I type my question, hit send, and hold my breath as I wait for an answer.

You aren't in one now, right? Wouldn't that be against the rules?

It would be, but I stopped working there a while back. And no,
I'm not with anyone.

Okay, this is promising. What if there's a chance for me?

Care to tell me why you quit?
Feel free to tell me to mind my
own business, though. :D

Am I using too many emojis? I feel like I am.

I met someone.

Well, screw me. Of course, he did. Someone who looks like he does wouldn't be single for long. I may as well wrap this up then. I'll call my sister and see if she wants to come over, eat chocolate, and wipe my tears.

Oh. Well. I hope the two of you
will be very happy.

That wasn't very convincing.

And then he sends the one that stops my heart.

I'm talking about you, Haley. I
met you.

What? Me?

I hop off the edge of the bed, jumping up and down and screaming like a toddler. I need to call Lindsey. We have so much to… Oh, wait. Eli (God, I *love* that name!) is likely waiting for a response.

What to say? My mind is racing at the possibilities of what he's saying. But I don't want to assume too much too quickly.

> That's very interesting… Tell me more?

> Storytime, huh? Okay, let's see… Once upon a time, a girl came into one of my scenes. I knew what I was supposed to do and say, but I was struck by her. She was the most beautiful woman I've ever seen, and I struggled to stay in character, to remember my lines. I felt an instant connection with her, and when our scene was done, I knew my time in the Club was over. I couldn't imagine touching another woman after touching her. Never wanted to kiss another woman after kissing her. I handed Piper my resignation the very next morning.

> Every day since, I've wondered about her, who she is, how I could find her but Piper refused to give me any information. I've dreamt about the way she responded under my hands, the way she felt tucked between my thighs. And the way her mouth tasted… Anyway, I saw her again purely by chance. It was like the gods heard me and granted my wish. And I'm hoping she'll say yes to a date with me. If she says no, well then, I may just have to convince her to change her mind by any means nec essary.

It's me. He's talking about me. As I read his text again and again, my tears flow freely, and I have to sit back down on the bed for fear I'll collapse. Long moments go by, and I memorize his words. Then, just in case, I take a screenshot for proof that this happened.

I'm re-reading his words, especially the 'any means necessary' part, for probably the ninth time when my phone chimes again.

> Uh, hello? Was that too much? I'm sorry if I went too far.

Dumbstruck, I'd forgotten to respond.

> That wasn't too much at all. I feel… the same. And I'd love to go out with you… Sir.

There's a long moment where nothing happens. I stare unblinking at the screen, chewing my thumbnail in anticipation, and then…

> Good Girl.

Chapter 32

A Scene Come True

*E*ight *months later…*

I stand in my brand-new kitchen and watch Eli haul in boxes, his thick muscles flexing with every step.

This is my favorite scene; one that I know I will never get tired of.

He dumps the boxes on the kitchen table and steps over to where I stand near the island. Without warning, he pulls me in for a rough kiss that leaves me breathless, just like his kisses always do. He releases me, slaps me on the ass, and goes back to work.

He disappears through the front door, and before I can even reach for a box to begin unpacking, his head pops in again.

"Hey, Haley?"

"Yes?"

"Love you."

"Love you more."

"Be careful unpacking the wasabi." He winks and he's gone again.

Our chemistry is out of this world, and every day with him is just as wonderful as the first. That's why we finally decided to move in together. I rented out my house, he gave up his lease, and we got a fantastic townhouse near the town center.

So far, it's been amazing. I hate to bring him up, but Eli is the opposite of Ben in every way and a perfect match for me.

Moral of the story?

If you ever find yourself invited to an exclusive, members-only Boyfriend Club, give it a shot.

You may end up in your favorite real-life book scene, where all endings are happy endings.

*** The End… ***
Oh, wait.. one more thing.

Chapter 33

Ben

I hate everything.

I hate this job. I hate this town. I hate my ex-fiancee.

My current situation is entirely Haley's fault. She *completely* overreacted to Sasha and me—that was just a fling! Every man is entitled to one last hurrah before getting married. Everyone knows that.

Then she just had to go and send that horrible, embarrassing picture to Mother. After that, my comfy, privileged life was over.

Just look at me. Disinherited and dishonored.

Thanks to Haley, Mother wrote me out of the will, claiming I'd never amount to anything. She told me in no uncertain terms that she was done with me and that I should never dare darken her doorstep again. My accounts were emptied, and my credit cards were canceled. How am I supposed to live?

Thanks to Haley, I had to get a job. Can you imagine? Me, who's never even pumped his own gas, as part of the working class?

Only, no one wanted to hire me because I'm thirty-two and have never actually held a job. Which is so stupid. I had a trust fund; why would I need a job? Ridiculous.

Thanks to Haley, I'm working at this shitty, run-down pawn shop as a "security guard." Security guard, my ass. They won't even give me a gun! The owner, an old, bald, grumpy dude, handed me a can of pepper spray instead. What am I supposed to do with that?

Then, when I tried to text Sasha, as a last resort, she blocked me!

As a final insult, this morning, my car wouldn't start and I had to take the bus. None of this is fair.

I hate everything.

The End